SOLO

Wishing you all
good things.

Debrah Bladen
XOXO,

Copyright

First Original Edition, October 2014
Copyright © 2014 by Deborah Bladon
ISBN-13: 978-1502791108
ISBN-10: 1502791102

Cover Design by Wolf & Eagle Media

SOLO

New York Times & USA Today Bestselling Author
DEBORAH BLADON

Also by Deborah Bladon

The Obsessed Series
The Exposed Series
The Pulse Series
The Vain Series
The Ruin Series
Impulse

ONE
LIBBY

"Have you fucked anyone in the chorus?"
This is when I wish like hell I'd brought my ear buds with me. Listening to this guy try to pick up Claudia isn't my idea of the way to spend an elevator ride early on a Monday morning. You'd think that landing a part in a Broadway play would mean work, work, and more work. It wouldn't mean the incessant sexual undertones that drive through every rehearsal and meeting day-after-day.

"No," she replies calmly.

"I wasn't talking to you," he snaps. "You. I'm talking to you."

Considering there are only three of us riding this slow ass elevator to the fourteenth floor I guess I need to address this. "Me?" I turn to face him and I feel an instant need to find my balance. I rest my hand against the chrome bar that stretches along the walls of the lift. He's hot. Like smoking hot as hell hot. Why didn't I notice him when I got on?

"What's your name?"

"Libby." This is one of those moments when I wish my parents would have given more thought to what I'd feel like being a twenty-two-year-old woman carrying around the name of a four-year-old. Libby? I've hated the name since I was in grade school. It screams sweetness and light.

"Libby?" he repeats it back. "I like it."

"What's your name?" I try to sound somewhat invested in this. I know his type. I've met dozens of guys just like this since I've moved to Manhattan. He's looking for a quick fuck. He's wearing an incredibly expensive three-piece suit and cuff links that cost more than my first, and only, car. I wouldn't be surprised if most women fall to their knees in his presence and give him and his dick exactly what they want. It can't hurt that he's got the most intense green eyes I've ever seen and jet black hair that is tousled enough to make him look that much more irresistible.

"You didn't answer my question." He takes a heavy step towards me as more people enter the elevator on the third floor.

I push back into the chrome bar, the coolness of it seeping through my thin t-shirt. I almost wish I would have worn something nicer to the rehearsal hall. Who knew I'd end up face-to-face with this? "What question?"

"Have you fucked anyone in the chorus, Libby?" His voice is deep and intimate. It's too intimate for such a small, crowded place.

"That's none of your business." I inhale the scent of his cologne. It's luxurious, subtle and intoxicating.

His hand darts to my waist as more people join the most interesting elevator ride I've ever encountered. "It's more my business than you know."

I roll my hips away from him. I can't want this man. I can't let any man tear my attention away from my work. "I doubt that," I whisper. "I really doubt that."

"Don't doubt me, Libby." He pushes his body closer to mine, the unmistakable firm outline of his cock pressing against my stomach.

I breathe a heavy sigh of relief as the elevator finally chimes its arrival on the fourteenth floor. "This is my stop." I try to push past him, but his hand holds firm to my waist.

"It's mine too." His right hand jumps to the wall behind me, trapping me in place. "Allow me to formally introduce myself before you run off."

My eyes dart over his shoulder to where Claudia is throwing me a confused look as she exits the lift. "I need to go," I say. "I can't be late."

"Don't worry about being late. I'm Alec Hughes."

"You're Alec Hughes?" I feel my breath catch. "You're the investor. You own my play."

"Correction, Libby." He leans in closer until his lips are almost touching mine. "I own the play. You work for me."

I feel all the blood drain from my face. I may actually faint. I've listened to one actress after another talk about Alec Hughes since I landed a spot in the chorus of Selfish Fate. This is supposed to be the next big musical to hit the Great White Way. It's also the proof that I've needed to show my parents that my decision to move to Manhattan to pursue a career in theatre has some merit. I can't blame them for doubting me. I'd invested years in getting a business degree in Denver and leaving right after graduation to come here did little to impress them. I'm now standing almost lip-to-lip with the one man who holds all the control for my future in his big, strong hands. They are the very same hands that are still trapping me in place.

"It's nice to meet you." My voice is rigid and alert. I know who he is now. We both know that I'm completely mindful of the fact that he's here for one reason, and one reason, only. This morning cuts will happen. People will be dropped before we move into previews. He's here to lower the gauntlet and from the energy pouring out of his body, he won't even bat a gorgeous, long eyelash when he whips people's dreams from under them.

His eyes charge over me before his hand snakes its way to my arm. "This way, Libby."

I follow his lead because there's no other choice. "Okay," I mutter under my breath. I can't walk into the rehearsal hall with him. I don't want that stigma attached to my face. I can't be that one woman he picks from the chorus line to fuck this season. I've heard the rumors. The innuendo isn't muted at all. Alec Hughes loves his women innocent, naïve and willing. He always leaves them in a pile of emotional dust after he's used them. My career is way too important to me. I'm not going to become the next name in his personal playbill.

"Mr. Hughes." The high pitched voice of the director, Sharma Newsome, pulls at my left.

"Sharma," he says sharply. "I'm busy."

"I need to use the…" my voice disappears into the air in the small hallway. I'm inches away from the ladies' restroom. It's the retreat I need. I'm going to bolt in there and with any luck at all, by the time I walk into the rehearsal hall, he'll have his sights set on someone else.

"I compiled a list of the candidates I like." Sharma pushes a piece of paper at Alec.

"Fine." He extends a hand to scoop it from her, pulling it into his fist without even the slightest glance.

I use the opportunity to make a dash to the restroom. I push on the wooden door, the creaky hinges alerting anyone else who may be in the dimly lit space. Being in the heart of mid-town, the building is showing its age, but it's a big, welcoming and enveloping space. It's the perfect retreat for everyone involved in the production of Selfish Fate. It's the space where my dreams are slowly coming true.

"You okay, Lib?" Claudia flips the words over her shoulder as she stares at me from one of the rectangular, chipped mirrors lining the wall just above a row of white, industrial looking sinks. "He looked like he was ready to fuck you right there between the ninth and tenth floors."

I blush at the image behind the words. If it was anyone else, I'd tell them to quiet down, but Claudia has been one of my best friends since I set foot in New York. She's brash, direct and has no filter. "That's Alec Hughes."

"You're obviously his pet project for the season." The words don't contain any emotion. There's no jealousy woven into them. Distaste isn't there either.

I pull a tube of clear lip gloss over my bottom lip. "I don't want to be."

She cocks a perfectly sculpted brunette brow in the mirror. "Why not? He's amazing. Did you see the way he looked at you? What was that?"

I had been pulled into him the moment he looked at me. He's the definition of everything any woman could ever want in a man visually. "I don't know what you're talking about," I lie. I have to lie. I don't want her to know that feeling Alec Hughes press himself against me has cleared my mind of just about everything, including my own name.

"You're a good actress, Lib. You're just not that good." The emphasis on *that* rips through me. "He was practically inside of you."

I laugh, not so much at the notion, but to bring some sense of lightness to the conversation. "I'm a great actress," I push back. I am. I'm not being egotistical. I don't throw the words out callously. I'm confident in my craft. That's why I'm here in the first place. I gave up everything to come here to pursue this dream. I know I have what it takes.

"You actually are." She reaches to push a wayward strand of my blonde hair towards the high ponytail I hurriedly crafted as I was racing towards the subway just a short thirty minutes ago. "Fix your hair."

I nod as I stare at myself in the mirror. I opted for no make-up again today. My brown eyes pop under my thick lashes enough that mascara is just a wasted expense. On a good day, or a date night, I'll opt for eyeliner and a tinted lip liner. Today I'm bare, exposed and hopeful that this won't be my last day preparing for my Broadway debut. "This is it." I turn to look directly at Claudia. "Good luck."

"I'm Irish, luck is part of me." She taps herself on the chest. "You don't need luck, either.

You've got Alec Hughes waiting outside that door for you."

"I doubt it," I chuckle. I do doubt it. By now, Alec Hughes will be in the rehearsal hall with another chorus girl pinned to the wall.

TWO
ALEC

What the fuck was that? I promised myself I wasn't going to fuck an actress in Selfish Fate. I'm here to cut the fat out of this production, not to seduce anyone. I'd blown my load down the throat of a waitress I met in Chelsea last night. She was eyeing me up over dinner so I gave her my number and picked her up when her shift ended. She had my dick out and in her mouth within minutes. That should have been enough to tide me over until I could find someone to fuck later this week. That pretty little blonde in the elevator changed everything. How the hell am I supposed to go into the rehearsal hall and sit down with my cock aching to be inside of that?

I can't keep doing this.

I can't stop doing this.

Just when I think I've got my cock under control I step into an elevator and see an ass like that. It's round, so plump and so tight. Those snug yoga pants she's wearing are doing nothing to hide that ripe, beautiful body she's trying not to display.

She dashed into the ladies' room when the director cornered me about the cast cuts today. I almost barreled right in after her. I can picture it now. I'd have her pressed against the wall, her ass right there as I rammed my dick into her from behind. I need to taste that. I have to have that. I don't give a fuck about being professional. I own this musical. She's part of it. I want her.

"Mr. Hughes?"

I turn to face the director again. I barely know the woman. All I know is that she's eager, hungry and she's going to get this musical into a theatre so I can finally recoup on at least one of my Broadway investments. This is the third production I've invested in and I've yet to see even a dollar back. I can't keep throwing money into this but I made a promise years ago. Sooner or later I'm going to have to fuck the sentimental shit and call it a day.

"What is it?" I blurt out at her.

She's taken back. I can see by the frown lines that instantly overtake her forehead. I don't care. I'm paying her a small fortune to get this production to where it needs to be. Her incessant calls over the last few days imploring me to come down here have worn on my last nerve. I don't have time for this shit.

"We need to make some decisions," she whines. "I need your input about the cast."

My eyes jut to the restroom. The pretty blonde is still hiding behind the door. I came on too strong. She looked like a little doe that was stuck on the railroad tracks when a train was speeding out of control. She's not used to men like me. I can tell she's never had a man like me before. That just makes her that much sweeter.

"I don't give a fuck what you do with the cast." I glance at my phone. I've got a full day of meetings. Running Hughes Enterprises is taxing. It sucks all of my time. The last thing I need is to be standing in this hallway talking about singers and dancers. I write the checks, I don't need to make every fucking decision. That's what the producer is for. Where the hell is he? Randall Myers should be here taking care of this himself.

"Excuse me?" Her tone is biting. I've offended her, obviously. Christ, the woman should be used to this by now. She's taken on an almost impossible job. We're trying to craft an entire Broadway production out of a book and musical score by two kids barely out of high school. The writers are literal unknowns. I've got nothing to back up their talent. It's like I'm climbing fucking Mount Everest with a bunch of children hanging from my back.

"You heard me." I stare at her. "I don't have the time to be called down here for meaningless shit like this."

"It's your play." She motions towards the doors that lead into the rehearsal space. "You should be interested in what's going on."

I open the door, allowing her to walk through first. "You should be handling all of this on your own." I survey the room, taking in the sight of all the dancers and singers who are betting their future on this production. Randall is nowhere to be found. This is the last production I invest in that has his name attached to it.

"You hired me and this is the way I do things." She takes a seat at a long, wooden table near the front of the space. "Take it or leave it, Mr. Hughes."

I scan the young women in the room as I lower myself into the chair next to her. Each of them catches my eye as I stop to take them in. There's no denying that every single one of them is worth a fuck. They've all heard about me. I can see it in their expressions. I don't want any of them though. I want Libby.

She's the one.

I'll have her in my bed by the end of the week.

THREE
LIBBY

"I want Libby."

They're just three words. They're small in relative comparison to other words but right now, they feel monumental. Every single person in the rehearsal hall has turned to look at me. I'm leaning against a windowsill, one hand fisted against my thigh. The other hand pressing against my stomach, trying with determined pressure to discourage my breakfast from making a return appearance. I feel ill. I'm so nauseous that I'm scared that I may actually fall forward, face first, onto the polished hardwood floors.

"You want Libby?" Sharma repeats back Alec's words, in a slightly louder tone than he used.

My eyes dart to Sharma. You'd think I'd crave the spotlight given my incessant need to perform every chance I can get, but right now, I just want everyone's gaze to fall to someone else. Why is this happening? I look like shit today. Why the hell is he doing this? I don't want to be that girl.

"Libby stays." He doesn't add anything to the two words. The twisted look of confusion on Sharma's face mirrors my own.

She shakes her head slightly as if to try to gauge some perspective. "You're saying you want Libby to stay in the chorus?"

Can they just shut the hell up about me already? I stand in the back with eleven other faceless dancers. Once this musical actually hits the big stage, I highly doubt that anyone without binoculars will be able to pick me out. This is the first step to what I hope will be a celebrated Broadway career. Right now I feel as though I'm teetering precariously on the edge of everything crashing down around me.

He nods slightly as his eyes skim the now smoothed piece of paper she handed to him in the hallway less than ten minutes ago. "Libby Duncan," he says my name slowly. "Libby Duncan stays."

"Fine." Her response is curt and exaggerated. I'm thankful she's tiring of his singular focus as much as I am. "What about the others?"

He takes one last lingering glance at the paper before handing it back to her. "Your choices are adequate. Fire everyone else."

There's a collective gasp in the room at his words. It's surprising to me, given the fact that we all are aware that some of us won't be here tomorrow. It's business. It's cutthroat and unless you have what it takes, you're going to be shown the door without any pomp and circumstance.

"I'll handle it." Sharma nods nervously as if she's convincing herself that she can take on the tortured task of crushing the dreams of almost half of the people in this room.

"Libby, a moment?" Alec pulls himself to his feet, his long, elegant fingers buttoning his suit jacket. "In the hallway."

I take a step forward hoping that my knees don't buckle. "Of course," I mutter under my breath knowing that every other woman in the room is now viewing me as the one that Alec Hughes has chosen to be his fuck buddy for the season. It may be what he wants but in my mind it's a role that I have no intention of playing.

* * *

17

I rehearse over and over again in my head what I'm going to say the moment he's done talking on the phone. I've been standing next to him now for five minutes. I'm fidgeting back and forth from foot-to-foot while I watch other dancers and singers exit the rehearsal hall as they make a mad dash towards the elevator. Some are holding in sobs, others are seething with anger and some just don't seem to give a damn.

"Libby?" Alec's hand is on my waist. "We need to discuss something."

"I'm not interested," I say evenly. "I'm flattered but I'm not interested."

A flash of a smile passes over his full lips. "What is it that you're not interested in?"

I run my index finger over the length of my nose. It's a nervous gesture that I've done since I can remember. "I'm not interested in being that girl."

"That girl?" He leans back against the wall, tucking his hands in the pockets of his pants. "What girl is that?"

I bite on the edge of my fingernail as I hunt for the right words. "The girl you choose."

"I choose a girl?" The suggestion of amusement in his luxurious deep tone isn't lost on me. "Tell me what I choose her for."

I'm blushing. I know that I am. It's not because I'm a virgin or my sexual experiences have been lacking. I'm blushing because he's asking me to repeat back all the sordid rumors I've heard about him. "You know what you choose her for." My intention isn't for my eyebrows to bounce around the way they are. I'm beginning to think I'm going to quash any interest he may have had in me just by the way I'm acting during this awkward conversation.

"You've heard things about me." The words leave his lips with a trail of assumption behind them. "I'd like to hear about that."

"There's nothing to tell," I lie. There's a hell of a lot to tell. I'm not one to spread gossip but when I'm sitting in a diner after rehearsals listening to other dancers talk about how he uses women, I'm not going to turn my head and ignore that.

"I'll fill in the blanks." He leans forward a touch. "You've heard that I select a young lady to be my companion for the season."

I nod. That's an elegant way to say he picks a fuck partner from the roster. "I've heard that."

"You think you're my pick for this season?" He cocks a brow.

My stomach instantly flip-flops within me. My heart starts pounding. "Yes," I whisper back.

"You're definitely intriguing." His finger jumps to my chin. "Before I make a final decision I need to know if you've slept with any of the men in the production."

I take a step back. The urgency to distance myself from him is overwhelming me. He's so comfortable asking me something incredibly intimate. "The answer is no even though it's none of your business. As I already said, I don't want to be that girl."

"You don't think you want to be that girl," he arrogantly corrects me.

"I don't want to be that girl." I find the words again and somehow they fall from my parched lips.

He adjusts the knot of his gray patterned tie as his eyes scan my face. "Don't be too quick to make a decision, Libby."

I stare past him to the weathered green and white wallpaper that covers the wall behind him. "I've already made up my mind." I can keep up the calm and collected demeanor for at least a few more minutes.

"Don't you think you should at least hear what I'm proposing?" he asks in an even, strong tone. "I think before you make a final decision you should know exactly what I'm offering."

There's no mistaking he's arrogant. It's not surprising to me. Manhattan is bursting at the seams with men who believe that they can offer women like me a ticket to something grand and life changing. I'm guessing in this case it's a thick, wide cock and some expensive dinners, likely in that order.

"No," I counter. "I'm not interested."

His lips purse as he takes in my answer. "Why not?"

I have to close my eyes to steel off the grin I feel coursing through me. It's obvious Alec Hughes isn't accustomed to being turned down. "You're not my type."

Libby, you are a liar.

"I'm not your type?" The surprise in his voice mirrors the expression on his face. "What's your type?"

I tap my index finger on my chin. "My type lives in the same building as me." It's not a complete lie. I've been flirting with Brandon, the man who lives down the hall from me, for weeks now. If I'm going to jump into bed with anyone in the near future, Brandon would be my first choice.

"You have a boyfriend?"

I smile at the inference. "He's not my boyfriend." He's not my anything actually. I don't even know his last name. All I do know is that he's likely never cornered a complete stranger to proposition her for sex in exchange for whatever Alec Hughes gives the women he sleeps with.

"I'm not following." His brow furrows. "If you don't have a boyfriend, why don't you take me up on my offer?"

"Mr. Hughes," I begin. I'm not typically someone who is stuck on formalities but I don't want there to be even an ounce of doubt about the nature of our relationship. I'm an employee of his. I don't want to become anything more than that.

"Alec," he corrects me. "Libby, call me Alec."

I nod. "Alec," I hesitate searching for the right words. Offending him isn't going to help my career in any positive way. He has way too much influence in this city for me to tell him to flippantly fuck the hell off. "I'm very flattered by your interest but I came to Manhattan with one goal in mind and I can't lose focus."

He adjusts his dark grey suit jacket, smoothing it against him. "I appreciate your dedication to your craft, Libby."

"Thank you," I interject. I know that he was going to add more. I know that he was going to say something alluring about the prospect of me being beneath his rock hard, gorgeous tall body. Maybe it's just my wishful thinking telling me that.

"Libby," he growls my name into the space between us as he steps forward. "I'd like to discuss this more but I have a meeting."

I open my mouth to tell him that the discussion is over but he's already stepping towards the elevator.

"I'll send a car for you after rehearsal." He juts into the open door of the lift and pulls his smart phone to his ear before I have a chance to say even one single word.

FOUR
ALEC

Goddamn it. She knows about me. Someone clued her in to the fact that I fuck a woman from every show I invest in. I was able to grab hold of the last two before they heard a thing about me. They saw me as the older, wiser, experienced guy who wanted to give them the time of their lives.

Libby is different. I could see the skepticism in her eyes. She's going to be a challenge.

"Lance, it's Alec," I bark into my smartphone as I walk through the doors of the building and into the pedestrian traffic on Eighth Avenue. "Get me everything you can find about Libby Duncan. She's on the payroll for Selfish Fate. "

I roll my finger across the screen ending the call.

"Mr. Hughes." I hear the familiar voice of my driver, Gabriel, pulling at me from the right. He's practically shouting above all of the traffic noise. "Over here."

I take a few large steps towards him as my phone chimes another call. "Hughes," I say into it, hoping that whoever is on the other end isn't going to ruin my mood.

"Alec." The smooth and sexy voice of a woman purrs over the line. "Where are you?"

"Britt?"

"It's me," she breathes heavily into the phone. "Can you come over?"

"Why the fuck would I do that?" I nod at Gabriel after lowering myself into the back seat. "My office," I mouth to him.

"Do I have to spell it out?" She's pouting. I can hear it between the words. "I haven't seen you in two weeks."

It's longer than that. I've been avoiding her. She's crazy as fuck. I took her to bed not more than a handful of times but she won't let go. "I told you I didn't want to see you anymore."

"You're lying." Her protest is marred by the crack in her voice. "You said I was fantastic."

I said a lot of shit I didn't mean when I was balls deep inside of her. "You're great," I offer back. I have to get her to drop the need. I can't keep towing her along. I don't want her. I need her to fuck off and I need that to happen today.

"Are you seeing someone else?"

It's a ridiculous question. I don't actually see anyone if we're going to dive into technicalities. I take women out because that's what they expect and need before they'll let me come down their throats. Having a girlfriend is out of the question. It doesn't fit into my life. "I'm not seeing anyone."

"What's the problem then?" Her tone is ripe with impatience. "You liked fucking me, didn't you?"

I can't lie. I can and I have but I don't see a purpose in lying about sex. "You're a great fuck, Britt."

"I'm wet right now thinking about your big cock."

She's not holding back. If I hadn't given everything I had to the nameless waitress last night I might be inclined to give Britt one last ride, but after seeing Libby today, my cock has one goal and that's to be buried anywhere inside of that body. "It's over, Britt."

"What's over? Our call? Do you have to go?" She's panicking; I can hear it pulling on the edges of the questions. "I can call you back later if you want."

I fucking hate this part. "We had fun but it's over."

"We are over?" She screams the words into the receiver. "We are not over, Alec."

"We are." I glance out of the window as we near the building that houses my offices. "I'm not looking for anything more."

"What the hell does that mean?" she barks the question out.

"It means I really enjoyed fucking you but I'm moving on." I slide across the seat. "Don't call me again."

* * *

"You're telling me that her father is Jensen Duncan?" I point at the chair in front of my desk. "Sit down."

"Libby Duncan's father is Jensen Duncan." Lance nods vigorously. "He owns the Duncan hotel chain."

"What the fuck?" I glance down at the growing pile of messages Lance collected for me while I was at the rehearsal hall. "I got this many calls when I was out?"

"More than that," he points out. "I handled a few on my own."

Does he want a fucking prize for doing his goddamned job? I'd hired a male assistant out of necessity, not preference. I'd bedded each of my last two female assistants and it got messy fast. Once the fun was over, I'd negotiated new positions for them with other divisions within the corporation. That meant one was working in our office in Los Angeles and the other in Chicago. Hiring a man was more cost efficient and it actually kept my eye on the prize. I'm getting more work done than I have in years.

"She's twenty-two. She has a degree in hospitality management." Lance continues, "I found out that she moved out here about a year ago. She fast tracked college after graduating from high school early."

"Early?" I push back. "Why?"

"She was in a private school in Colorado." His eyes scan a paper in front of him. "She's gifted."

"Gifted?" Her ass is a gift to the universe. I'll give her that.

"Her IQ is off the charts." He shrugs. "How do you know her anyways?"

"I don't know her…" I point towards my office door signaling for him to leave. "I'm about to know her very well."

I run my thumb along my smartphone pulling up a number before the sound of a phone ringing fills the air. "This is Gabriel." He answers on the first ring.

"I need you to go back to the building in mid-town this afternoon." I search my desk for one of the documents I need for my meeting that begins in less than five minutes. "It's the same building you just picked me up at."

"I know the one, sir."

"I'll send you a picture of a blond woman." I push my chair back from my desk. "She should be done by four. She's expecting a car to pick her up. Bring her to the condo on Central Park West. I'll be there waiting for her."

"Yes, sir."

I push the screen to end the call before I scroll through the saved photos stopping to stare at the ones I took of Libby this morning as she was waiting to board the elevator to go up to rehearsal space. She hadn't even noticed me standing a few feet away from her capturing picture after picture of her perfect face and gorgeous body. I stare at the curve of her breasts and the softness of her hips as I send one of the pictures to Gabriel.

I glance at the time, grab a pile of documents off my desk and head back out the door. If all goes well I'll have my head buried between her legs in the next six hours.

FIVE
LIBBY

"This is the subway, Lib." Claudia sweeps her hand around the crowded train. "Why are you on the subway when he said he was sending a car for you?"

It's a valid question. I don't think I can provide an answer that would make any sense to her or to Alec Hughes. "I have nothing to say to him."

"You have nothing to say to him?" She parrots my words back at a decibel level that's high enough to wake sleeping dogs. The way many of our fellow commuters crane their necks to look at us suggests they're more invested in this conversation than I am.

"I told him I wasn't interested," I say the words without any emotion. This is actually the third time I've explained all of this to Claudia since we left rehearsal. I hadn't brought it up until we were on the platform waiting for the train. I'd noticed the dark sedan parked right outside the door of the building the moment we stepped into the cool afternoon air. I had steered her away from it without a second glance.

"I think there was a car waiting there." She skims her eyes over the ceiling of the train as if she's going to pull an image of the street into her mind. "I saw a car, Lib. He's going to be pissed at you."

"He's not." I laugh before tapping my hand over her forearm. "I'll bet you that he already has another girl lined up."

"Five dollars?'

"What?" I pull my eyes from a young mother and her son who are sitting on the edge of one of the crowded benches. "What's five dollars?"

"I'll bet you five dollars he hasn't lined anyone else up." She holds out her hand.

I grasp it within my own and shake it vigorously. "You're on. I'm not sure what I can buy for five dollars in this city, but I'm going to win that bet."

"I'll win." She brushes her hand over her shoulder. "I can taste sweet victory already."

I laugh at her obvious confidence. "What are you doing for dinner tonight?"

"I have a date." The huge smile on her face doesn't match the lack of exuberance in her tone.

"I can't tell if you're happy about that or not." I lean in closer as another new wave of commuters push themselves into the already crowded space.

She whips her hand through her short brown hair. "I don't know. He hits all my credentials but there's something about him that's a little off."

My curiosity races to the surface. Since I met Claudia at an audition just over a year ago, she's become one of my most trusted friends. She's not shy when it comes to sharing details about the men she sees. "Off in what way?" I ask even though right now I'm not all that interested in what she does or doesn't see in her latest conquest. Judging by her incessant need to talk about being married before she's twenty-five, I'd bet that every guy who hears about the wedding dress she already has picked out, runs for the hills.

"I don't know." She tips her chin in my direction. "Call it women's intuition."

I nod towards the door as we near our stop. "I'm going to have a hot bath and order in tonight."

"Another exciting night in the life of Libby Duncan," she teases as she pushes me out of the train's door and onto the subway platform.

* * *

"This is totally inappropriate." I pull the tattered pink robe around me. "Jade isn't even here."

"I'll sit and wait for her." He motions behind me to the mismatched furniture that sits in the middle of our small living room. "She'll be back soon, right?"

"Joey, you two broke up weeks ago." I push back on the door. He's tall, slim and much stronger than I am. "She doesn't want you around here."

"Listen, Libby, I'm not going anywhere." He shoves harder and I feel my grip on the door loosening.

I can't let him in. My roommate, Jade, broke up with him after she caught him sexting with another girl. At first glance, you'd think that Jade would be every man's dream. She's a model and her looks back it up. She's at least six feet tall, her face is flawless and her body slim and toned. I knew when I interviewed her to be my roommate that all the insecurities I felt about myself would race to the surface. They have but since I've gotten to know her I've seen the implausible façade of what she presents to the world crack. She's been cheated on by the men she's loved more than once, and Joey is just the last in a long line of men who've wronged her.

"I'll call the police." It's a threat that has no merit. I won't do that. I'm not going to jump into the middle of Jade's love life just because Joey feels badly that he sent some random woman a picture of his naked dick. She told me last night that she's considering getting back together with him. How can I have his ass hauled off to jail? The only thing he's guilty of is being a cheating asshole.

"No you won't." He doesn't even hesitate as he calls my bluff.

"Joey, just go." I drive all my weight into the door. "She's not here. She's at a shoot right now."

He's unrelenting. "Either you let me in or I'll sit out here and wait."

I twist my hand around his wrist in a calculated move my father taught me before I boarded the airplane that brought me to New

York. "You're not coming in," I seethe as I finally yank his arm away and slam the door shut.

I heave a hefty sigh of relief and lean back against the door. I can hear him cursing behind the wooden barrier that now separates the two of us. This isn't the first time I've had to forcibly keep one of Jade's many suitors from entering the apartment. I need to talk to her about it as soon as she gets home if I can wrestle a moment of her time away from Joey, that is.

My planned evening of eating potato chips and watching movies in my pajamas has come to a screeching halt. I need to get dressed if Jade is going to drag Joey's sorry ass into this apartment. Damn my life. I knew I should have rented my own place. Sitting in my room for more than an hour makes me stir crazy. This apartment is tiny but it's my home so I'm going to make the best of it.

I hear a very faint knock on the door just as I'm pulling on a pair of oversized sweat pants and a t-shirt with my high school football team's name emblazoned across the front. These are the comforts of home and I wear them when I'm feeling like I don't quite belong in this big, sometimes very emotionally empty, city.

"Go to hell, Joey," I call through the door. "Go home. I'll tell her you were here."

The volume of the knocking only increases. The rat-a-tat-tat grows increasingly louder with each rhythmic beat. I reach for my smartphone and pound out a message to Jade telling her that Joey is determined to talk to her.

I slump against the door, wondering if I'm ever going to get to sleep tonight.

SIX
ALEC

She didn't show up. She fucking didn't get in the car that I had sent for her. Goddamn. I'd waited at the condo for more than an hour while Gabriel raced around the streets of Manhattan trying to hunt her down. There's no way in hell that she didn't know that car was for her. She walked past it on purpose. She actually decided to avoid me. It's rare. I admit that most women fall over themselves trying to get my attention. When one doesn't want it, it naturally makes my cock ache for her.

I call Lance's name the moment I step off the elevator and into the space that houses my offices. Heads turn when I pass and it has everything to do with the fact that I hold their fate in my hands. I run this business the same way I run my entire life. I'll drop you if you prove that you're not essential to me. I've had to fire more people than I can count since my father gave me control of his business. His idea of keeping employees loyal was giving them bonuses and tropical vacations. Mine is using security software to track their online movements and cameras in every office to see who is fucking who on my dime.

Where the hell is Lance? I pick up my desk phone just as he pops his blond head around the corner and into my office. "I'm sorry, sir. I was busy."

"Busy?" I unbutton my suit jacket before lowering myself into my chair. "Busy doing what?"

"I was helping someone with the coffeemaker."

"There's a coffeemaker in this office?"

"In the lunch room, sir."

"Where's that?" I cock a brow. Obviously my time in the office is actually spent in my office not wandering the halls trying to make friends.

"It's down the hall. You need to take the second left and then…"

"Christ, I was joking, Lance."

He pulls his lips into a goofy grin and I swear I get a glimpse of a retainer in his mouth. How old is this kid? "What do you need?"

"When you were checking on Libby Duncan, did you happen to get an address for her?"

He nods vigorously. "I thought you might want that."

"Why would you think that?"

"Why would I think what?"

Lance is smarter than that. "Whatever, Lance. Do you have it or not?"

"I have it." He bolts to his feet. "It's at my desk."

"Write it down for me. I need to pay Ms. Duncan a visit tonight."

* * *

I don't come down to this neighborhood often. If I'm being completely honest, I don't come down here ever. I'm here tonight for only one reason and with any luck it's still wearing those yoga pants it was earlier.

I've been thinking about Libby all day. The way she looked up into my face when I told her who I was keeps flashing through my mind. She was both intrigued and intimidated.

The fact that she didn't immediately agree to sleep with me isn't surprising. People, mostly women, will tell you that I can have any woman I want with the snap of a finger. It's not true. I have to work for it sometimes, but never too hard. If a woman can't see the value in what I'm offering, there's always another waiting around the corner.

Tonight, I'm here to find out if Libby is as smart as Lance says she is. If she is, this will be the last time I have to come down here. Next time I see her, she'll be on her knees, in my condo with my dick sliding between her lips.

Since there's no fucking elevator I take the steps two at a time until I reach her floor. The minute I round the corner towards her door I see him. It's a guy, Libby's age. He's tall and slim. He's pacing back and forth, his hands pulling on his hair. What the fuck is this?

"Hey," I call out to him.

"Hey, dude." He tips his hand in my direction.

"You waiting for someone?"

"Jade."

Jade isn't Libby so what the fuck ever.

I walk up to her door, knock softly on it and listen for her footsteps.

There's only silence so I knock again, louder this time and wait for the moment when she finally opens the door.

SEVEN
LIBBY

He won't stop knocking. Why did I pick a roommate whose entire life is drama filled? All I want is to go to bed.

"Fuck off." I slam my hand against the faded white paint that covers the door. "Just fuck off already." This night has fast become a living and breathing nightmare.

"Libby?" A male voice that's deep and smooth pours through the air. "Libby Duncan?"

I know that voice. I'll never forget that voice. It's the same voice that propositioned me just hours earlier. Alec Hughes, in all his handsome and desperately alluring glory is standing on the other side of my apartment door.

What now? Am I supposed to just open the door and let him in? I can't do that. I look even worse now than I did this morning when he was pressed up against me in the elevator.

"Libby?" He repeats my name in a low growl. "I'd like to talk to you."

I'd like to disappear into thin air.

"I'm busy," I call back in a desperate attempt to get him to leave. I want him to leave, don't I? My heart is racing within my chest but that's because of what just happened with Joey. It has to be. I don't want Alec Hughes. My body might want him, but my career focused mind is telling me that it's a bad idea to open the door and let him in.

Fuck. It.

I swing the door wide open and I have to take a step back. He's beautiful. How can a man look this good after an entire day at the office? He's changed his clothing. He's wearing dark pants and a light green v neck sweater. His black hair is still a tousled mess but now he's sporting the first hints of a five o'clock shadow. Considering that it's after nine, he looks better than most men do when they first shower and shave for the day.

"Wow," I say without thinking. Libby, you said that out loud. You fucking just said that to him.

"Wow?" He repeats it back as he steps forward. "What's the wow for?"

I need to pull myself together. "I thought… it's just that…I thought you were someone else," I stammer through gritted teeth. This is going nowhere near the way I want it to. I want to appear at least semi coherent.

"You thought I was the guy wandering the hall." He tosses his head back to the side as he steps over the threshold into my apartment.

"He's still out there?" I dart my head out into the hallway and catch a glimpse of Joey's back as he walks down the corridor. "I told him to leave."

Alec turns to look at me. "I'll remove him from the building myself if he's bothering you."

The declaration catches me off guard. It's a strange mixture of old fashioned chivalry with an off putting assumption.

"He's harmless," I say as I shut the door. "He's waiting for my roommate."

"For a moment I thought he was your type." His gaze is focused on my t-shirt.

There's no way he can believe I have even an ounce of fashion sense. So far today he's caught me twice in outfits that shouldn't ever see the light of day. "My type?"

"Earlier you said your type lives in this building." He taps his black loafer against the floor. "I assumed that was your type." His hand flies past my head towards the door.

"You thought Joey was my type?" I crack a wide grin.

"That's amusing?" He rakes his hand through his hair.

"He's my roommate's ex-boyfriend," I offer. Why am I telling him this? Why is he even here?

His eyes survey the entire room. "Do you like living here?"

The judgment beneath the question is glaringly obvious. He doesn't approve. "It's comfortable," I snap. I can't even begin to conjure up an assumed image of what his place must look like. Judging by the fact that he's the sole backer of Selfish Fate, I know that he's not pinching his pennies the way I am.

He nods as his eyes drift back to me. "You didn't get in the car I sent for you today."

I purse my lips together. I didn't anticipate having this conversation with him. I assumed that once he realized I was serious about not wanting to be his temporary distraction that he'd move on to someone else. The chorus is filled with beautiful women. "I took the subway."

"I told you I wanted to speak to you." He pushes his hands into the pockets of his pants. "I want to explain a few things to you."

I'm tired. I have an early call time at the rehearsal hall tomorrow and then a shift at the jewelry store I work at a few times a week. I don't have time to banter about the merits of being the puppet on his string. I don't want to become someone whose only legacy in the theatre world is that she jumped into the bed of Alec Hughes.

"I don't have time for this," I spit out. The words sound more rushed and aggressive than I want them to.

"You have plans?" The corner of his mouth pops up as his hand grazes across my hip. "Are you going to work out? Do you mug people at night? What plans do you have dressed like that?"

I try not to break a smile. I know I look hideous. "I'm going to sleep."

He pulls up the sleeve of his sweater to look at his watch. "You're going to bed at nine o'clock?"

"Yes." I nod heavily. "I have a busy day tomorrow."

He scrubs his hand over his face. "This won't take long, Libby."

I know I should insist that he leave and it's not because I'm craving the lumpy mattress that this furnished apartment came with. I'm worried that he's going to find a way to climb over the wall of resistance I've built around myself and convince me to become his fuck buddy for the season. "Please have a seat." That sounded just like my voice. I felt my lips moving. Did I just invite Alec Hughes into my apartment? My fucking mouth did and now my mind has to fight against everything I want to stay in control.

EIGHT
ALEC

"You want me to agree to spend time with you while I'm in the production?"

I nod before crossing my left leg over the right. "That's it, Libby."

Fuck this piece of shit couch I'm sitting on is uncomfortable. I swear to God there's a stray spring piercing my left nut. Her father is a goddamned billionaire and she lives in this hell hole? What's up with that? She's got to be one of those trust fund kids out to prove to her parents that she can make it on her own, rats and all.

"That can't be it." She sounds confused. "I'm not an idiot."

She's a genius. Most of the women I fuck can't string together a complete sentence. *Wait.* That's a lie. I don't talk to them long enough to know whether they have a grasp of basic vocabulary or not. When I'm staring at a woman's mouth I'm not thinking about the words coming out of it. I'm usually focused on my dick going in it. "Why can't that be it?"

"I have to give you something in return," she says sheepishly.

She's shy? I highly doubt that. She's an actress. They're never shy. She's pussy footing around the issue. She wants to ask if she has to blow me when I take her out to a nice dinner or if I'll sit her in my lap so she can ride my cock when I give her a set of earrings. Come on, Libby, spit it out.

"Your company is all I'm asking for," I shoot back.

Her eyes jut around the room. She's actually thinking about it. Maybe driving over here wasn't such a waste of my time after all.

"That's bullshit," she whispers.

"It's bullshit?" I wait a breath before I continue under a sly grin. "Why is it bullshit?"

She blows a puff of air out between pursed lips. "You want to sleep with me."

Hell, yes, I do. Actually, I don't want to sleep with her. I want to drive my cock into her and then send her home. Although, personally I wouldn't call this hole in the wall a home.

I cock my left brow. "I can't fault you for wanting to cut right to the chase."

She sighs. I can tell that she's frustrated. She's fidgeting in her seat. "I'm sorry," she offers in a breathless tone.

Fuck me, she's gorgeous. Even wearing what looks like her boyfriend's clothes she's hotter than most women I've ever been with.

"I'm a direct person too, Libby." I lean forward to rest my elbow on my knee. "It's a strong quality. I like it."

"Alec, I," she starts before pulling in a deep breath. "I don't sleep with men I don't know. I don't sleep with men in exchange for anything."

There it is. The resistance I felt the moment I touched her in the elevator. I dart my gaze to the floor before I pull it back to her. "You're very focused on the sleeping together part of this."

She blushes slightly as if she's realizing I haven't mentioned fucking her. "I know that has to be part of the arrangement."

"Arrangement? I don't see it as an arrangement." I don't. I'd label it a lot of things, but not an arrangement. That speaks of a formality that I don't want. I want to fuck her, over and over again. Then I want her to leave me alone and go on with her life. End of story.

"It's an arrangement. I've heard about it."

"You've heard rumors about it," I counter as I lean back again. "You don't have a clear picture of what I'm offering you."

She rubs her hand over her forehead. Anxiety is pulling her brows together. "I know that you choose a girl from every production you invest in."

"Not every production," I snap back in a lie. "Not every woman I see is involved in the theatre."

Give me more credit than that. I fuck women. I'll fuck any woman who catches my eye. I don't have a type. It just so happens I fucked two who were in the Broadway plays I invested in.

"You have propositioned women in other plays you've backed, haven't you?"

My brow furrows. She hasn't just heard the stories about me; she's jumped to her own conclusions. "You're coming into this with a preconceived notion of who I am."

"I can tell you exactly what I've heard about you if you want." She crosses her arms across her chest in defiance.

She's a firecracker. I haven't worked this hard to get a woman into my bed, well, ever. Why the fuck am I still sitting in this dump listening to her cast judgment on me? What's wrong with me? I can be in a bar within the next ten minutes with at least three women lined up who want to get me off.

"Please do," I say even though I know I'm going to regret this. "I'm all ears."

She adjusts herself slightly on the edge of the chair she's sitting on. "I heard that you picked a girl to sleep with from the last play you invested in and the play before that."

I raise my index finger to stop her. "Libby, I already told you…"

"I know," she interrupts. "You don't choose a woman from every production." The clear emphasis is on the word *every*.

I nod in response. My eyes are glued to her face. I'm taking way too much pleasure in watching her squirm.

She pinches the bridge of her nose. "You do nice things for them."

Nice things? Seriously? What the fuck is that?

"I take very good care of the women I spend my time with."

Her face flushes at my words. She knows I'm not talking about gifts or outings. I'm talking about sex. I take care of my partners. I never leave them wanting. Correction. I never leave them unsatisfied. I always leave them wanting more.

"I'm sure you do," she says softly.

"Libby." I run my hand along my cheek, stopping to race my finger over my chin. "You're very attractive." I know I should follow my instinct and walk out the door right now, but I can't. There's something about her that is pulling me into her. I don't need to define it right now. All I need is to get her to agree to this.

She glances down at her clothing before pulling her hand through her hair. "I'm not."

"You're interesting to me," I offer, ignoring her comment. There's no way in hell she's oblivious to how attractive she is. I don't buy that for a second. "I'd like to get to know you better."

"We can just go on a date," she suggests.

"I want more than a date." My tone is forceful. "I'm a busy man. I don't just date women. I like if we have a clear picture of where things are headed before we invest our time in each other."

"Is that because of expectations?" For someone who is as smart as Libby is, she definitely knows how to play the dumb blond card to a tee. She's playing with me. She has her own agenda.

"Let's cut to the chase." I'm tired of this cat and mouse game we're playing. Right now, I actually have no idea, which one of us is the cat and which is the mouse.

"Okay, fine." She pushes both her heels into the floor. "What are you actually proposing?"

I've never had to spell it out with this much definition. Christ, she's wearing on my last nerve. "You make yourself available to me over the course of the next few months and in return, I'll help your career."

Her brow spikes at the mention of her career. I threw that in there for good measure. If pressed in the past, I would have offered a piece of jewelry or a car. Yes, I'm that guy. I'm the guy who buys a woman the pretty, fancy shit she wants so I can get a taste of her pussy. Judge me not. The approach has yet to fail me.

"Help my career in what way?" Her interest is not only peaking, it's exploding. I just found the magic ticket to get inside Libby Duncan's ripe, beautiful body. I just have to give her a chance to shine in Selfish Fate and she's mine.

"We'll work on the details of that later," I offer. Later, as in, when I've figured out what the hell I can do for her career. I know I can cement a speaking role or a solo in Selfish Fate for her. I'm the one footing the entire bill for that train wreck.

She tilts her chin to the left as her big, brown eyes rake over my face. "Do I have to fuck you?"

Hearing that word flow from her gorgeous, plump pink lips wakes my cock up. I'm instantly hard. "Do you want to fuck me?" It's a rhetorical question. I already know the answer.

Her shoulders rise as she pulls in a very slow, sensual breath. "I'm not sure."

My dick goes limp, my blood pressure rises and I search the ether for something to say back to that. "You're not sure?"

She twists her lips together in a pout. "No, I'm not sure," she repeats silencing any arousal I may have felt.

What the fuck kind of game is she playing? I'm literally speechless. I need to get the hell out of here. "I'll pick you up for dinner tomorrow at eight."

Her eyes dart to the floor before she responds, "I can't tomorrow. I have to work."

I pull myself up to my feet. "You don't have to work. Rehearsal ends at four," I point out.

"I have another job."

"Where?" I bite back. Why am I even bothering at this point? There were at least five other women in the chorus I could have in my bed later tonight.

She studies my face for a minute as if she's running an internal debate about whether or not to confide in me. "I work at a jewelry store."

"Doing what?"

Her eyebrows bolt up in surprise. "What do you think? I sell jewelry."

I need a fucking drink. "You're in a Broadway play, Libby. Why the hell are you working in a jewelry store?"

"I like it," she tosses back before she bolts to her feet. "I need to go to bed."

I need a redo of this entire day. Fucking Libby Duncan is proving to be more challenging than most of the million dollar deals I've got under my thumb right now. There isn't a woman alive that's worth this much trouble.

NINE
LIBBY

"Are all men in New York arrogant assholes?" I ask, after turning to make sure no customers are lingering in the store.

"Jax isn't an asshole." My boss, Ivy, leans forward on the glass display case. "Wait. He was a little bit of an asshole when I first met him."

I roll my eyes as I place a diamond bracelet in the case. "I don't believe you. Jax is a prince."

"He's a prince now," she says through a small chuckle. "When we first met, he was a jerk."

It's hard to place the words in my reality. Ivy's husband, Jax, has been nothing but kind to me since I started working at her jewelry store, Whispers of Grace. He'll often come in with a coffee for each of us if I work the Saturday morning shift. He's the one who encouraged me to go on the audition for Selfish Fate.

Although he isn't an actual owner of the store, he's here a lot. I can see how much he loves his wife every time he steps through the door.

"I want to find a guy like Jax." I smile up at her. "You're really lucky."

She nods. "I know that I am."

"My schedule is going to change once the musical goes to previews," I begin. "I might have to quit."

"Quit?" She quips, obvious disappointment laced into the word. "No, Libby. You don't have to quit."

"I might not have time to be here anymore."

"Then we'll consider it a leave of absence." She moves away from the display case after grabbing a pair of ruby earrings. "I want to add to these. I should take them up to my studio."

I nod. Ivy's such a beautiful person, both inside and out. She puts a touch of her soul into every piece that she creates in her studio upstairs. Jewelry is her passion as much as performing is mine. When I first walked into her store a year ago, it was to look at her designs. She offered me a part-time job on the spot and I haven't looked back since. She and Jax have helped me feel as though I have roots in New York. They treat me like family.

"Can I talk to you about something?" I blurt the question out without much thought. I was going to bring this up with Claudia earlier, but there's no way she can have the same detached perspective that Ivy will.

"Sure." She turns to look directly at me. "Is something wrong?"

"No." I shake my head a bit too vigorously.

I've been fighting my own inner demons over this issue all day. I can't stop thinking about Alec Hughes and the conversation we had in my apartment last night. My sex had ached when he'd left and I had to bring myself to orgasm just so I could fall asleep.

"It's a guy thing, isn't it?" She reaches her hand across the case to cover my own. "I can help. I'm good at relationship stuff."

I'm taking her word for it. She's one of the few people in this city that I know who is in a happy, seemingly balanced relationship. I'm not looking for that for myself just yet, but I need to hear someone's opinion on Alec's proposition.

"Is it someone you're dating?" Her voice peaks with the question. I can tell she's obviously interested in what I'm about to tell her.

I scratch my chin. Once I say this, I can't take it back. She'll hold the knowledge and she'll share it with Jax. I can't blame them if they judge me for it. I'm judging myself for even considering it. I can't quiet my curiosity. I want to go out with Alec Hughes. I want to get a better understanding of what he's offering to me. I just don't want to be that girl who sleeps with a man to further her career.

"No," I say the word slowly. "It's someone that I work with."

"It's someone from the play." She claps her hands together as if she's about to open a treasure box. This is gossip to her. I can see it within her expression.

"It's the man who invested in the play," I correct her. "He's backing the entire production."

"Alec Hughes?" His name leaves her lips in a heated rush. "You have something going on with Alec Hughes?"

How? How the hell does Ivy know his name? "You know about Alec?" Using his name in such a casual way feels foreign to me. It speaks of an intimacy that isn't there. I'm not sure I want it to be there.

"Jax knows him. They're friends I think. I met him once."

"What?" That's more of a *what the fuck* than a what but I want to keep my job.

"Let me think." She taps her index finger against her forehead as if she's lodging free some tidbit of information that is stuck within her memory. "Jax has a best friend. His name is Hunter Reynolds. Have you heard of him?"

I shake my head slowly. How did we go from my wanting advice about Alec's overt sexual proposition to her talking about her husband's bestie? "No."

"He owns Axel NY." Her hand flies to her chest. "The food there is to die for."

Now we're going to talk about restaurants? I should have just asked Claudia her opinion on this. I don't respond because when Ivy's on a tangent, the best thing I can do is hold on for dear life and go along for the ride.

"Hunter is married to Sadie Lockwood. You'd like her."

I'm sure I would but what the hell does this have to do with Alec? I open my mouth to say something but I've got nothing. Thankfully, Ivy isn't done yet.

"Alec is friends with Sadie and Hunter. That's how Jax met him." She scratches the top of her head. "He's very good looking."

I need to back pedal within the conversation. "Who is good looking?"

"Alec Hughes." Her head darts around the empty store. "Don't tell Jax I said that."

I shrug my shoulders. I'm so lost right now that I feel as though I need a road map to lead me out of the maze that is Ivy's mind. "I won't," I say as a courtesy. How the hell would I even bring this up with Jax? I don't even have a clear picture about what the two of us are talking about.

"What's going on between you and him?" she asks in a barely there whisper.

I stare at her. I can't tell her a thing. She knows who Alec is. Keeping secrets is a foreign concept to Ivy. "Nothing," I say through a stilted laugh. "Nothing at all."

She tilts her head to the side. She's not buying what I'm selling at all. "Are you dating him?"

I grip the edge of the display case. I need the anchor to get me through the rest of this conversation. "No," I scoff in the most believable way I can.

"Good." She pats my hand. "I don't think he's good for you."

I don't ask her to elaborate. I don't need her to. I need to forget about Alec Hughes.

TEN
ALEC

She was talking about me. I was falling asleep during the conference call I had with Jax Walker and Hunter Reynolds about the prospect of investing in their new restaurant venture and then Libby's name was thrown into the mix. I had no fucking idea she worked for Jax's wife. Knowing she asked Ivy about me has set the wheels in my brain turning again. I may have a chance with her yet.

I've been trying to forget her since she practically pushed me out of her apartment a few nights ago. I'd gone to the gym after that encounter. I had to work off all the pent up energy that was racing through me. I'd thought about picking up someone to fuck, but I couldn't get the image of Libby out of my mind.

"Sir, you have a meeting in ten minutes." Lance pops his head around the corner and into my office. "Are you ready for that?"

I'm ready to fire his ass. I can't tolerate when anyone second guesses me, even if it's my assistant. I pay him well to make sure that I'm at the top of my game but I don't tolerate foolish questions like whether I'm prepared for a meeting. I've been working at my father's company since I graduated from college, seven years ago. I'm one of the youngest CEOs in Manhattan.

"Lance, get in here." I motion for him to shut the door behind him.

A flash of concern dodges his expression. "What is it, sir?"

As much as I'd revel in watching him plead for his job, I need him too much to toss him to the curb at this point. "I spoke to an old friend earlier. His name is Hunter Reynolds."

"The Hunter Reynolds who owns Axel NY?"

Apparently I'm paying Lance enough to eat there. I need to check on that. "That's him."

He nods before jotting something down on his legal pad. Who does that anymore? Isn't that what a tablet is for?

"I need you to make a reservation for me there for tomorrow night." I shuffle through a few papers on my desk looking for a contract that I need to take to my meeting.

"Tomorrow night?" he parrots back. "I heard it takes months to get a table."

I drop my hands before I turn my face to look directly at him. "It doesn't take months for me." It sounds cocky. I'm cocky. It fits.

"Do I say it's for you?"

I really need to check on Lance's salary. Did he seriously just ask me that?

"I mean…" he stammers. "I just meant are you dining alone?"

"What to do you think?" I tilt my chin up.

"I think it's for two." The corner of his mouth twitches.

"Eight o'clock."

"Consider it done." He jumps to his feet before he slides out the door and into the hallway.

With that taken care of there's only one more slight detail I need to tend to. I want Libby Duncan's perfect ass in the chair across from me at Axel tomorrow night.

* * *

"You've been thinking about me," I say the words smoothly the moment the elevator doors open on the fourteenth floor. It's precisely four o'clock. I'm here to convince her to have dinner with me tomorrow.

Libby's head darts up just as her feet stop in place. Everyone behind her bottlenecks and she's thrown forward in an instant. I reach out to try and steady her as she drops into the car and onto her knees.

I stare down at her for what feels like an eternity. Sweet Jesus. Is that what she's going to look like on the floor of my condo before she wraps her gorgeous pink lips around my dick?

"What?" She reaches behind her as if she expects one of her cast mates will help lift her to her feet. "What did you say to me?"

I take a full step forward as I raise my hand warning them all to stop. "Take the next one," I bark at them.

They acquiesce. It's not as though they have another choice. Each of them knows exactly who I am. I push the button for the lobby just as the doors close.

"Don't bother helping me up." There's no masking the sarcasm dripping from the words. She's clawing at the wall of the elevator, trying to gain some sense of traction.

I don't move. It's not that I'm a selfish and inconsiderate bastard. It's that I'm stunned by the way she looks. Her blonde hair is tied loosely into a ponytail, although half of it has fallen out around her face. She's wearing a light blue tank top and apparently a black bra underneath judging by the strap that is falling onto her shoulder. The very tiny black skirt she has on is inching higher with every single movement she makes. I can't take my eyes off of her.

I watch in silence as she adjusts her skirt once she's on her feet. Her hands pull her hair completely free of its restraints. The long blond locks tumble free. Christ. She looks like she's just been fucked. She's a sweet mess.

"Why are you here?" she throws the question at me without following it with even a slight glance.

"Look at me, Libby," I order. I'm not going to play any games today. We are not going to have a repeat of what happened in her apartment the other night. After seeing her today, I know what I want. I don't see any reason to not be open and direct. We're wasting precious time.

"What?" she asks in a mix of a whimper and a whine. "What do you want?"

I charge towards her grabbing both her shoulders in my hands. I push her back until she's resting against the elevator wall. The low moan that escapes her travels straight to my cock. I can't stop myself. I won't stop myself.

"You," I whisper the word against her lips. "I want you."

ELEVEN
LIBBY

The elevator jars to a hard stop when it reaches the lobby of the building. He steps back as his hands drop from my shoulders. Damn my life all to hell. He said he wanted me. I heard him. He was just about to kiss me and now he's standing at least a foot away from me.

Maybe it's fate. Maybe my initial reluctance to stay away from him was right. I'm just another conquest to him. I don't need that complication in my life right now. I have to stay focused on my role in the musical. It's why I came to New York in the first place.

The doors fly open and several people rush in before either Alec or I have a chance to get off. I push through them. I don't feel as though I can breathe in this tiny space. I need air. I need to get outside and onto the street.

"Libby, wait." His voice is behind me as I make a rush towards the glass doors.

"I can't," I mutter under my breath. "I can't."

I know it's impossible for him to hear me in the crowded space. I doubt that he can even see me. It's late afternoon and many of the people who work in the offices are clearing out for the day. It's congested and I'm grateful for the reprieve from the intense moment we shared in the elevator.

"Stop." The word hits me an instant before his hand is around my waist.

I try to break free but any effort I'm putting in is in vain. It's almost as though I'm in a struggle by myself. I'm twisting recklessly and he's standing behind me, almost motionless. "I need to be somewhere, Mr. Hughes."

His grip on my waist doesn't lessen as he guides me through the glass doors of the building and into the street. "I'll take you anywhere you need to be."

Even though I know that getting into a car with him is a mistake I'm likely going to regret the moment it pulls away from the curb, I do it. I do it willingly. I crawl into the open door of the same sedan that was idling by the curb the other day. I slide across the seat so Alec can sit next to me and I stare out the window as I hear the car door slam. This is it. This is when I tell Alec Hughes to go straight to hell.

*   *   *

"As much as I'm thoroughly enjoying this random drive around the city, Libby, it would be helpful if you could supply an address of the place you need to be."

It would be helpful if you weren't as good looking as you are. How am I supposed to resist him when we're sitting this close together?

"When you were in my apartment the other night, you said that you could help my career." I take a slow breath to quiet all the anxiety I'm feeling. My lips feel as though they're still back in that elevator waiting to be kissed by him. "I'd like to know exactly what that means."

His hand is resting leisurely on the back of the seat. His chest heaves slightly before he turns his face towards me. "It means I have the ability to open a few doors for you."

That clarified absolutely nothing at all. "Can you be more specific?"

His mouth thins into a serious line. "I'm funding the entire project, Libby. I do have some say in the production."

I want particulars. It's not going to change my mind about hopping onto his dick, but I'm curious. I want to know exactly what Alec Hughes would do to get me into bed. It's completely and totally about perceived value. I'm curious about where I rate on his scale. "You must have something in mind that you can offer to me."

"There are many things I can offer you, Libby. I was thinking about a solo."

"You would get me a solo if I sleep with you?" I ask the question while staring at his face, looking for clues about how serious he is. This can't actually be real. I've heard about the infamous casting couch. This wasn't how I pictured it at all.

He leans forward, his fingers flitting past the bottom of my hair before they land on my chin. "Is that what it's going to take to get you into my bed?"

He actually is as big of an asshole as everyone says he is.

"Mr. Hughes," I stress his name wanting to make it abundantly clear that the two of us are in a business relationship and nothing more. "Mr. Hughes, if I wanted to get into your bed, I would do so because I wanted to fuck you, not because you promised me a solo or anything else."

He closes his eyes just as a soft curse falls from his mouth. "Libby, we're both adults. I'd like to have sex with you. I'm reasonably sure you'd like to have sex with me. I can make it worth your while if you agree to spend time with me during the run of the play."

"I don't sleep with men for favors." I point out.

"I can change the entire course of your career, Libby." His fingers pull on the bottom of my hair. "I can make you a star."

I'd be lying if I said that it isn't tempting. From where I'm sitting, with a very full and clear view of how impossibly handsome he is, I can't honestly see a downside to this. I get a chance to stand out from the rest of the actresses in the chorus and I get to have sex with the most attractive man I've ever laid eyes on. Why am I not saying yes to him? Oh, wait. It's because it would make me a whore.

"It would mean I'm a whore." That's what happens when I speak before I think. "I mean, I don't have any problem with a woman doing what she needs to do to make a dollar or to get a leg up in the world, but I can't do it. It's just not who I am." Aren't you a fucking angel, Libby? No wonder he's staring at you like you have three heads attached to your neck.

"What if I took sex out of the equation?" His tongue flits over his bottom lip.

My panties are officially wet after watching that. "What? No sex?"

"I didn't say forever." His chin lifts. "Let's start with one dinner. You agree to go to dinner tomorrow evening with me and we'll take it from there."

"Just dinner?"

"Just dinner, Libby. No strings attached."

TWELVE
ALEC

Who the hell was that in the car with Libby Duncan? Did I actually agree to take sex off the table? That may have been the most fucked up thing I've ever done. I almost had her in the elevator. She was practically waiting for me to kiss her and then she took off the minute the doors opened. Christ, this one may be more trouble than she's worth. I shouldn't have to work this hard to get any woman.

That's exactly why I'm at this club. It's in the heart of Times Square and there's a hotel an elevator ride away. It's what every man's fuck pad dreams are made of. I paid for a room in Hotel Aeon as soon as I walked through the doors. Now I've got my drink in my hand, a clear view of the club's entrance and a pocket full of condoms. If I fuck someone tonight, Libby Duncan becomes just another girl in the chorus line. This insatiable need I'm feeling isn't about her. I'm here to prove that to myself.

I watch the steady stream of women entering the club. I can have my pick. It's a sea of blondes and brunettes with an occasional redhead tossed in the mix to throw the balance off. I scan the faces of each as she enters. Not one of them is doing anything for me or my dick.

I want a blond with full lips. I want a nose that perks up just at the tip. I want brown eyes that are big, wide and full of desire. I want Libby.

Fuck me all to hell. I have to get her out of my mind.

"Hey." It's almost as soft as the tap on my shoulder.

I spin around. She's acceptable. Brunette, tall, and curvy with gorgeous blue eyes and a dress that's two sizes too small. "Hey," I parrot back.

"Will you buy me a drink?"

If it's going to get me laid, I'll buy you ten. "Sure."

"I'll have a screaming orgasm."

"When you finish your drink, I'll see to that myself." I raise my glass of bourbon in her direction. "Now, tell me what you're drinking."

She throws her head back in laughter. "I meant I'll have a screaming orgasm martini. You're funny."

You're not that bright. "I aim to please." In more ways than one, I might add.

"What's your name, handsome?"

"Charlie," I toss out because I don't want to hear her screaming my name out when I'm devouring her cunt. "What's your name?"

"Lucy."

I don't care if it's real or not. Lucy is going to help me forget that Libby Duncan even exists. "Drink up, Lucy. I promised you a screaming orgasm and I'm ready to deliver it."

I can't say for certain but I'm vaguely aware of my mouth hanging open as she takes the martini from the bartender, raises the glass to her lips and downs the entire thing in one mouthful. "I'm ready, Charlie."

I'll say she's ready. This night just got a hell of a lot better.

* * *

"You don't think I'm pretty, do you?"

I cross my arms over my head and lean back into the pillow. "That's not it at all, Lucy."

She stomps her bare foot against the carpeted floor. Her fake tits don't move an inch. I can't take my eyes off of them. "What is it then?"

It's a good question. I'm on this bed, naked, limp and staring at a gorgeous naked woman who is ready to fuck me to my dick's content. "I've got a lot on my mind."

"Like what?" She takes a step forward and her tits still don't bounce at all.

I pat the side of the bed. If she wraps those lips of hers around my cock we may be able to get this party started. I can't remember the last time my cock didn't jump to attention in the presence of a naked woman. I can't remember because it's never fucking happened before.

"Do you want me to put that in my mouth?" She nods towards my cock with a look of fear in her eyes.

If she thinks it's intimidating now, she should see it once it's ready to start taking prisoners or pussies. "Don't look so excited, Lucy."

She pulls her lips back over her teeth. This is quickly turning into a freak show or a horror show depending on which side of my dick you're on. I'd bet money on the fact that Lucy doesn't like sucking cock.

"It's not that…I mean I want it inside of me here but not there." Her hand floats over her crotch before it lands on her lip.

Correct me if I'm wrong. Fifteen minutes ago I was in a club with hundreds of women who would have my cock all the way down their throats by now and I have to pick the one who thinks it's revolting. When did my sex life because so fucked up? When?

"You can just put the tip in your mouth." I lift my limp, yet impressive, dick into my palm. I hold the head gingerly between my index finger and thumb and try to hypnotize Lucy with it. "Just try it."

"No." She's on her feet again. "I can't do it. It's disgusting."

Limp dick, I'd like to introduce you to even softer cock. Can this get any worse?

"I'm a virgin," she blurts out at the top of her lungs.

Christ, I am living in a fucking nightmare right now.

"You're a virgin?" I bark at her. "You're a fucking virgin?"

She tries to cross her arms over her chest but her ridiculously oversized, rock hard tits are in the way. "I came here to have sex."

"No." I stand up and brush past her. "You shouldn't be here having sex."

"Why not?"

I pull my boxer briefs on before doing up my pants. "I'm not the kind of guy you should be losing your virginity to. Don't you have a boyfriend?"

She shakes her head. "I can't find one. I thought these would help."

I don't know why I bother to look up but I do. Lucy's got her tits in her hands like they're two rockets about to launch into the universe. They are definitely locked and loaded.

"You're not from New York, are you?" I'm trying here. I really am. I don't want to sound as completely pissed off as I do right now.

She throws her lip into a pout. "I'm from Alaska."

"Alaska?" I slip my suit jacket over my shoulders. "What the fuck are you doing here?"

"I quit school. I want to be a model."

Unless she's planning on being the after model for a boob job gone wrong, her modeling career isn't going to float regardless of how large her tits are. "A model?"

"You even said I was pretty, Charlie."

I feel a migraine coming on or a shitload of regret, but I'm going to say it regardless. "Give me your number, Lucy. I'll set you up with an interview with an agency."

No. I'm not doing this because I think she has a shot in hell. I'm doing this so that she stops wasting her time chasing a dream that's never going to happen. If someone in authority, in the business, tells her it's not her golden ticket, she'll hopefully drag her ass back to Alaska and go back to school.

"You're the best, Charlie."

I don't have any time to react before she's on her feet with her arms wrapped around my neck. I'm standing in a hotel room, with a beautiful woman clinging to me and all I can think about is the way Libby Duncan looked in the elevator today.

THIRTEEN
LIBBY

"How do you feel about sucking cock?"

"I don't see that on the menu," I say before I look across the table at him. "What's in that? Pig?"

He smirks and runs his fingers along the side of his cheek. "Me."

I have to look away so he doesn't see the blush that runs over my face. I don't even know what I'm doing here. I picked up my phone at least ten times today bound and determined to call this dinner date off. I'm not even sure it's a date. I don't know what it is or what I'm doing here.

"Have I told you that you look beautiful, Libby?"

He's exaggerating. I look average. I'm wearing a black shift dress and black heels. I pinned my hair up because I ran out of time after rehearsal and I couldn't style it the way I wanted. If I had to judge by the smile on Alec's face when he picked me up to bring me to Axel NY, I'd say I look good. I'm not putting too much weight into that though. The sucking cock question was all the proof I need that he's still focused on one thing and one thing only.

"You said that sex was off the table." I tap the table for good measure.

"I didn't say talking about sex was off the table," he retorts, his palm hitting the table's edge before he takes another bite of his food.

"Have you ever been sued for sexual harassment?" I pick up my salad fork and stab a carrot.

He stops mid chew to stare at me. I watch in silence as he swallows hard. "No. Why would I be sued for sexual harassment?"

Is he shitting me? I would have guessed that he has a team of attorneys on retainer to deal with all the women he sleeps with that he also works with. "You proposition women you work with to sleep with you." I want to add a 'duh' to the end of that, but he did bring me to one of the nicest restaurants in the city so I'll refrain, for now.

"Every woman I've slept," he pauses. "Every woman I've fucked has been a willing participant."

"That's because you gave them all something." I scoop up a piece of lettuce before putting it in my mouth.

He reaches for his wine glass, downing the remainder of the Cabernet Sauvignon that was there. I've watched my father enjoy the finer things in life for years and I know, for a fact that the bottle of wine Alec ordered for the two of us is more than most people can expect to make working an entire week. I also know that he didn't do it to impress me. It did though and I've already enjoyed two full glasses.

"I'm a generous person, Libby."

I can't refute that. I did a search online for him last night. He's a philanthropist in addition to being one of the wealthiest men in Manhattan. He is active in his support of many charities. There were dozens of photographs of him at events with children, hospital patients and homeless people. If I hadn't seen the images myself I would never have believed that the man doing all that good work and the guy sitting across from me are the same person.

"I know. I read about that." My tongue darts over my lips.

"Where did you read that?" The grin on his face makes him look both cocky and completely seductive.

I scratch my nose. Why did I tell him that I read about him? Now he knows that I'm interested. Shit. "It was in a magazine or something. It was a long time ago." Nice save, Libby.

"You've been researching me." He nods as the waiter refills his wine glass and then mine. "You were asking about me at the jewelry store too."

Thanks a lot, Ivy. Way to rat me out.

"My boss, Ivy, told me you know her husband," I try to say without seething.

"We're acquaintances," he offers. "We share a mutual friend. He's actually the owner of this restaurant."

Of course he is. Alec Hughes knows every important person in this city. I, on the other hand, know a handful of people who have absolutely no influence in New York at all, including the guy in Central Park who always winks at me when he sells me a pretzel.

"Back to my original question." He spins his fork in the air as if that's going to send us back in time. "Do you like sucking cock?"

"I can't tell you how many ways that is completely inappropriate," I spit out. "It's demeaning and it objectifies women."

"If you asked me if I like eating pussy I wouldn't be offended at all."

I have to grasp the side of the table to steady myself. "We're trying to have dinner. This isn't the kind of conversation you have at dinner." There's no way that didn't make me sound like a prude.

He carefully places his fork next to his plate, moves his wine glass over a half of an inch, reaches across the table and tugs my hand into his before I can react. "We are two adults who are having an adult conversation about sex, Libby. This isn't Sunday school. I like eating pussy. I want to eat your pussy until you scream my name over and over again. Now, answer the question. Do you like sucking cock?"

My breath is caught somewhere between my chest and my mouth. I can't take my eyes off of him. I can't get the image of his head buried between my legs out of my mind. "I…I…" I stammer because my sex is clenching so tightly that I fear I may come.

"Do you like having a big, hard cock between those pretty pink lips of yours?"

I nod slowly. I run my index finger over my bottom lip knowing full well the impact it's having on him. I open my mouth and whisper in a heated rush. "I love sucking cock. I love it."

FOURTEEN
ALEC

Goddamn my entire life to hell. I'm reasonably sure my dick is going to explode right here in the middle of Axel NY. It has never been this hard before. Ever.

"Did you hear me?" She leans forward so far her breasts are pushed together and spilling out of the top of her dress. "I said that I…"

"Libby," I practically shout her name. I can't hear her say the words again. I will seriously blow my load inside my very expensive pants. "I heard you."

"Okay." She shrugs her shoulder, which only serves to make her tits look that much more inviting. "You didn't say anything when I answered the question."

What the fuck was I supposed to say when she answered the question? I want to tell her to crawl under the table and prove that she loves it. I want to take her out to my car right now and sit her on my face so I can eat her sweet cunt. I want her in my bed. Christ. I have never wanted a woman more than this.

"Alec? Alec?" The voice pulling me out of thoughts of Libby riding my face is way too low to be hers. It's a man's voice. How fucked up is my life this week?

"Hunter." Excuse me if I don't get up to greet you but I have a raging hard-on. "This is Libby Duncan. She's an actress in the musical I'm investing in."

He reaches across the table to shake her hand. She grins at him, tilting her head to the side. I hear her talking about Ivy and Jax. Her lips keep moving and more words are coming out but I can't make them out. I'm too focused on the curve of her neck and how round her breasts are. Her hair is falling out of the messy bun she tried to put it in. She's so imperfect that she's perfect. Everything about her is beautiful to look at.

"Alec?" Hunter's hand is on my shoulder. "Are you alright?"

I rub my hand over the front of my pants under the shadow of the linen tablecloth. I'm finally calming down. Jesus, I feel like I've been on a rollercoaster. "I'm good."

"I was just telling Libby that we've known each other for years." He pats me on the back.

"Yeah, years," I offer. "We go way back."

"What was Alec like back then?" Libby smiles up at Hunter and I feel a pang of jealousy wash over me. I want that smile. How fucking romantic does that sound? I'm the definition of pathetic right now.

"You don't want to know," I interject because I don't want Hunter hanging around. I want him to get the hell away from our table so we can get back to talking about how much Libby likes sucking cock, particularly my cock, while hopefully she'll become much better acquainted with tonight.

"He's always been like this." There's no mistaking the deep chuckle in his voice as he sweeps his hand over my head.

Fuck you too, Hunter.

"I love the food here." Libby points at her half-eaten, incredibly overpriced salad. "The chef is excellent."

"Do you want to come back to the kitchen?" He reaches a hand in her direction. "They're making up some tasting plates for new menu items for next week. I'd love your opinion."

What the hell, Hunter? What the hell?

"You can meet my wife, Sadie. She's back there right now."

Libby's on her feet before I can say a thing. She teeters momentarily, wobbling slightly on her heels before Hunter scoops his hands around her to stop her from falling face first into the table. When the fuck did this go from talking about my dick in her mouth to Hunter practically grabbing her tits?

"Are you coming, Alec?" Hunter calls back over his shoulder as he guides Libby through the crowded restaurant.

"No," I spit back under my breath. "I doubt I'll be coming at all tonight."

* * *

"Your friend is nice."

Your ass is nice.

"He's a good guy." I glance out the window of the car. Hunter is a good guy. I can always depend on him. Tonight I depended on him to fuck up my date.

"Are you okay?" Her voice is soft. Christ, it's so soft and warm.

I twist my head back around to look at her and I catch my breath. She's pulled her hair out of the upsweep. It's falling around her shoulders. "You're beautiful, Libby."

She tilts her head down slightly but I see the blush that runs over her nose and onto her cheeks. "You say that to everyone."

Guilty as charged. Women love hearing they're beautiful. I tell them because it's true. Every woman is beautiful in her own way. With Libby it's different though. She's different. Everything about her is breathtaking to look at.

"Not everyone," I correct her with a smile.

"Tonight was…" her mouth twists slightly as she pulls her bottom lip between her teeth. "Tonight was…well…I'd have to say it was…"

"It was fun," I say it more as a fact than a question. I don't know what the hell tonight was. After she'd gone back into the kitchen I'd sat there alone at the table for more than thirty minutes. When she finally reappeared all I wanted was to get the hell out of there. I need to go home and jack off. I'm on the edge and looking at her isn't helping at all.

Her hands clench slightly in her lap. "Yes, it was fun."

"Did you just admit to having fun with me, Libby?" I know it's immature but I want to hear it again.

"I've never been in the kitchen of such a nice restaurant before." Her hand reaches out to tap mine. "Thank you for taking me there."

Thank you for making me want you more than I can fucking stand right now.

"Have you thought about spending more time with me?" I would wait to bring it up but we're only a few blocks from her excuse for an apartment and I don't want to miss my chance.

She rubs her index finger over her right eye causing a trail of mascara to appear on her cheek. It somehow makes her that much more desirable. "I have thought about it."

Don't stop there, Libby. Spit it out. Only this one time though. She has to swallow. Jesus. How fucking hot would it be to watch her swallowing my load?

Alec, get a fucking grip.

"Did you make a decision?" I ask, trying to keep my voice from giving away all the anxiety I'm feeling. How can I be so hung up on her? She's just a woman.

"I have." She pulls the ends of her hair between her thumb and index finger twisting it around. "We're here now."

My head bolts out the window and I realize Gabriel just turned the car onto her street. "What did you decide?"

She turns slowly until she's facing me directly. "I want you to kiss me."

"You want me to kiss you?" I repeat back certain that there's no way in hell she said that to me.

Her eyes scan my face as she inches closer to me on the seat "Yes, I want that."

"I want it too," I say. Of course I fucking want it.

My eyes don't leave her face as she slides across the seat. I'm frozen in place as she twists her body until she's in my lap facing me. I can't breathe as her soft hands cup my face and I moan aloud as her beautiful lips glide over mine.

FIFTEEN
LIBBY

This is why I don't drink expensive wine any-more. I end up doing things I shouldn't. Right now, I'm sitting in Alec Hughes' lap making out with him.

"Let me come up to your apartment," he growls the words into my mouth. "Please, Libby."

I rub my wet panties over his suited crotch. I can feel how hard his cock is. I can feel how big his cock is. Is that why he's so cocky? Is there a direct link? I had too much wine.

I don't answer. I dart my tongue into his mouth, running it along his. One of his hands is on my lower back, the other on my thigh.

"Libby," he says through a whine. "I want to fuck you."

My sex clenches when he says the words. It's what I want too. I don't know who I'm try-ing to fool by pretending I don't. I almost came in the restaurant when he was talking about tasting me.

I lean back slightly so our lips part. "Sometimes when I drink too much wine I get aroused."

His brow cocks slightly as a grin takes over his gorgeous mouth. "I'll take note of that."

"At the restaurant you said some things about my body." I nod towards my panties. "It was hot."

"You liked it?" I feel his cock jump in his pants so I adjust myself, pressing my mound into him.

I push my hair back from the side of my face. I must look ridiculous. "I touched myself until I came in the bathroom."

"You what?" His hand races up my thigh to the edge of my panties. "Did you say you came in the bathroom?"

My index finger darts to my mouth. "I wasn't going to say anything. It's a secret."

"Christ, Libby." His lips are pressed against mine. "I need to be inside of you."

I lean back just far enough that I can breathe. My lips are almost touching his. "What happens if we have sex?"

"You'll have an orgasm. Actually, you'll have more than one."

"No, that's not what I meant." I drag my pussy across his pants. "You're really good in bed, aren't you?"

Both of his hands are on my thighs now. "I've never had a complaint."

I press my lips into his again. His kiss is lush and open. His breath trails down my neck as one of his fingers darts into my panties. I can't stifle the moan that escapes me. I'm so grateful that Gabriel got out of the car once he parked. I can't imagine the sounds he's heard coming from the back seat of Alec's car.

"Libby, God, you're so smooth." His finger runs the length of my folds, parting them slightly. "I want to taste you, Libby. I want my tongue inside of this."

I want that too. I've wanted that since he talked about it at dinner. It's the reason I had to go into the washroom at Axel NY, hide in a stall and make myself come. I couldn't stand the intensity of what I was feeling. I can't stand it now.

"I feel so…" my voice trails as he slides his finger over my swollen clitoris.

"Take me upstairs, Libby," he whispers the words into my neck. "I need to taste you."

I nod. I can't say the words. I don't want to give voice to everything I'm feeling. I don't want to hear myself confess that my body is aching to have his inside of it. I just want to feel. I just want to enjoy the pleasure he's going to give to me.

"Gabriel," he barks the driver's name out as soon as he opens the car door. "Help us out of here. I'm taking Libby upstairs."

* * *

"I don't want you to get me a solo." I don't hesitate when I hand him the keys to my apartment. "I don't want to complicate things."

He puts the key in the lock and swings the door open, pushing me inside. "What do you want if you don't want a solo?"

I try to look at his face but he's too busy undressing. Technically, he's only taking off his suit jacket but he's starting to work on his cuff links so it's only a matter of time before I get to see Alec Hughes completely nude.

I might as well get comfortable too seeing as how it's my apartment. I throw my purse on the floor before I grab the hem of my dress and pull it over my head in one single movement. I've seen it done in movies. It's sexy as hell. In my case, it's awkward as fuck. My hair catches on one of the buttons that runs down the back. I whimper aloud because it stings. I'm stuck in a darkness of my own making which is really just the inside of my dress, which is now sitting on my head.

"Libby?" The low grumble of a chuckle is there. It may even be a muted laugh.

"Are you laughing at me?" I turn towards where his voice emanated from. I can only see a small sliver of light shining above my head.

"Your body is beautiful," he says softly. "You look amazing, Libby."

Sure. Right. I'm standing in heels, with a matching set of black panties and bra on. That's all well and good but the god dammed dress that is stuck over my head isn't adding to my sex appeal in the least.

"Help me, please." I can't believe I actually have to say it. Is it not obvious that a little assistance may be appreciated? I may have to take 'gentleman' off the checklist I had running in my head of all the things about Alec I liked.

"Shit. I'm sorry," he mutters at me through the darkness. "I'll pull it off."

I wince as he gives the dress a strong tug. I almost cry out as when he jerks on it again, pulling a lock of my hair out with it. "My hair," I whimper.

"I'm sorry." His hand jumps to the side of my head. "I didn't mean to pull out your hair."

I look at his bare chest. My eyes glide over his shoulders up his neck to his face. "Wow," I mutter beneath my breath. "Wow."

"You like what you see?"

I might be panting at this point. I don't even know. He's so muscular. He actually has a six pack. I've never seen one this close before. I'm so tempted to drop to my knees and run my hands all over it, but if I do that he's going to open his pants and then I'll want to…

"Libby? Are you okay?" His hands are on my waist pulling me into him.

"You smell nice." I tap his rock hard chest with my palm. "I mean you smell so nice. What is that?"

He scoops me up in his arms in one easy movement. He's romantic. He may pretend to be all about fucking but he's romantic. He's carrying me to my bed so he can make love to me. He's chivalrous. He's nothing like I thought he would be. Nothing. I…

SIXTEEN
ALEC

Hey, Karma. You can fuck right off.
She's asleep. She fell asleep when I was carrying her to her bed. This is how the universe is paying me back for fucking so many random women. I finally find one I actually like being around who happens to also be the hottest thing I've ever seen and she's almost naked and fast asleep.

When did this become my life? I've never had a woman fall asleep on me. I've also never had a woman get her dress stuck over her head. That was fucking adorable. She has no idea what she's doing to me.

I hear a door slam. It has to be the roommate. I remember Libby telling me her roommate's ex-boyfriend was stalking here in the hallway the first night I came over. I carefully pull a sheet over Libby's body before I run my lips over her forehead.

"Who are you?" Her voice assaults me the minute I close the door to Libby's room.

I turn to look at her. She's tall, brunette, chiseled features. She's a model. I've seen her somewhere before. "I'm Alec. Who are you?"

"Jade." Her eyes move from Libby's door to my half-dressed body. "What were you doing with Libby?"

Not what I wanted to be doing. "Libby's asleep. I'm leaving."

"You can stay."

It's there in her voice. I've heard it dozens of times before. It's the want and the need that comes from a woman who isn't satisfied. Libby's roommate is actually making a play for me. I don't want her living here anymore.

"I just walked out of your roommate's bedroom," I spit the words out at her before I turn to walk towards the door. I need to get dressed.

"So?" she purrs back. "You look like you can go more than one round."

"I'm not interested," I say with conviction. I'm not interested. Normally, I'd have in a woman like her bent over a chair with my cock giving her everything she could ever possibly need. Right now, I'm debating whether

I should go back in Libby's room, strip down and fall asleep with her wrapped in my arms.

"I won't tell, Libby." She shoves at my shoulder as I pull on my suit jacket. "She'll never know."

"I'll know." I shake my head, turn the doorknob and step out into the hallway.

* * *

"White roses. I want two dozen of them. I'll text the address to you and sign the card, Alec. That's Alec with a 'c' not Alex with an 'x.' I want them there within the hour." I swipe my thumb across my phone ending the call.

It's seven in the morning. Libby will be leaving for rehearsal by nine so with any luck those flowers will get to her before she walks out the door. I tap out her address and send it in a text to a florist I found on Google. I'm normally not the flower sending type.

"Mr. Hughes?"

I don't need to turn towards the doorway of my office to know that Lance is standing there. He's supposed to be here at eight with a coffee in hand. It's seven. What the fuck is he doing here? I came here to think and now I have to deal with that?

"You're here early, sir. Do you want me to get your coffee now?"

"Right now," I turn around sharply.

"Is something wrong?" He takes a step into my office.

I don't recall offering that invitation. "Get the coffee."

He races out the door almost tripping over his own feet. I'll give him credit for being enthusiastic. Not credit in the form of a raise, mind you.

My desk phone rings and I immediately decide to ignore it. No one knows I'm here and the fact that they're calling this early doesn't impress me one bit. I'm all for making the most of your day, but I'm not sure I'm ready to start mine officially yet. It finally comes to a stop almost the exact moment my cell starts ringing. Persistence is a quality I admire. I recognize the number immediately.

"Margaret," I say her name clearly into the phone. "Good morning."

"Alec." Her voice is calm. It's completely different than the last time we spoke. "I tried calling you at your office."

"It's just past seven here." It's a conversation we've had time and time again. "New York lags a few hours behind London."

"Right." The word is clipped. "I'm calling about opening night."

I knew the call was coming. I've been avoiding it and her. Whenever I've backed a new play it meant seeing Margaret and David. The experience was rarely pleasant, but always painful.

"We want to book our flights before prices go up."

"I'll arrange all of that for you." I always do. There hasn't been one time when Margaret and David have come to New York where I haven't paid for the entire trip. She knows it. She's always sure to remind me of it.

"Are you sure, Alec?"

I hesitate briefly before answering. I'm tempted to just tell her what I'm feeling. They don't need to come back here. I don't need to keep investing in plays. This needs to be over. "I'm positive."

SEVENTEEN
LIBBY

"Those are for me?"

I know I shouldn't sound so completely shocked, but let's be realistic for a minute. I live with a budding supermodel. Her legs are almost as long as my entire body. Her face is exotic and flawless. Since I've lived with Jade every single flower delivery has been for her. On her birthday, there was literally no room to move. There were dozens of bouquets being delivered all day. Now, today, the day after my so-called-date with Alec Hughes, I'm the one with the flowers. They're beautiful.

"That guy that was in your room last night must have sent them." She points the half peeled banana in her hand at them. "He was hot, Libby. Score."

No, I didn't score. I didn't even round third base. I fell asleep. "You saw him?"

"He was coming out of your room half-dressed." She takes a big bite of the end of the fruit. "I said goodnight to him."

Why do I suddenly have a vision of Jade pulling Alec into her room to give him a good-night kiss on his dick? "What does that mean?"

She cocks one of her perfectly coiffed dark brows. "What do you think it means?"

My head hurts too much for this. I need to shower before I go to rehearsal. I also need to find my dress. "Have you seen my dress, Jade?"

"You left it on the floor." She nods her head back towards the front door. "If I was with a man like that, I'd strip naked as soon as I could too."

I turn around to go back down the hall-way. I can't be late for rehearsal. I need to get my mind back into my job. I didn't work this hard to lose my chance to finally make it on Broadway. Today I turn a new leaf. I need to forget about Alec Hughes and what it felt like to kiss him.

* * *

"I didn't think it was possible for you to look more beautiful than you did last night." His voice floats over my neck as I'm reaching down to pick up my bag.

I was prepared to face him in a day or two. I can't do it now. I don't even know what I said or did last night. I know I kissed him. I can't forget that but everything after that is a blur. I stay hunched over hoping that someone else in the rehearsal hall will say something that will steal his attention away from me.

"Mr. Hughes," Sharma says his name over my shoulder. "I'm glad you're here. I wanted to talk to you about a few things."

I straighten my back. This is my chance. I can walk out the doors and hop into the elevator while he discusses business with the director. I'll be able to regain some of my misplaced composure and face him when I don't feel so completely hung over and embarrassed.

"Not now." His hand catches my elbow. "I'm busy."

"These issues aren't going to sort themselves out." She's frustrated and growing impatient. I've heard the very same inflections in her voice when the cast hasn't performed a scene exactly the way she's instructed us to.

"Call my office and make an appointment. I'll be happy to talk to you about things there."

Her footsteps storm out of the room with all the measured grace of a herd of wild horses. I can hear others moving around behind us. The almost whispered references to Alec and I are apparent even if they aren't overt.

"Did you get the flowers, Libby?" His lips brush against the back of my neck.

Turning around, I look up into his beautiful face. His brow cocks in anticipation. "I got the flowers, yes. They're really beautiful."

"I'm glad you like them." He leans back, jutting his hands in the pockets of his pants. "How are you feeling today?"

I run my tongue over my top teeth trying to chase away how dry my mouth feels. "I'm okay. I'm sorry I got drunk."

"You weren't drunk." His hand leaps from his pocket to push a hair back that has fallen onto my face. "You didn't eat enough dinner. The wine got the best of you."

He's polite and understanding and incredibly hot. His eyes are so green. I exhale as I pull my gaze from him to the floor. "I fell asleep."

"I put you to bed."

I'm grateful that he whispers the words under his breath. I've already been subjected to the jealous glances of other dancers in the chorus. They know that I'm the girl that Alec Hughes has chosen this season. I'm still not sure I want to be. I trace the nail on my right thumb with my left one. "We need to talk about things."

"We do?"

I nod. "I have to work at the store tonight. I need to go but can we talk soon?"

He reaches for my elbow again. "I'll have Gabriel drive us. We'll stop at your apartment so you can change. Then we'll take you to the store."

I pull away. I can't do it. I can't talk to him today because I don't know what I'll say yet. "Not today. I'll go myself."

I turn and walk out of the rehearsal hall. By the time I board the elevator, he's still not in sight.

EIGHTEEN
ALEC

I'm losing her. I haven't tasted her yet and I'm already about to lose her. I saw it in her eyes. It was there. Regret. I see it when I look in the mirror every fucking morning. I'd recognize it across a football field. She regrets what we did the other night. She regrets climbing onto my lap and kissing me in a way I've never been kissed before. She regrets the whole goddamn thing.

I was tempted to drive to the jewelry store to beg her to give me a chance last night but I don't beg women for anything. If she wants to walk away, I'm not going to drop to my knees and promise her I'll be something I'm not. There's no fucking way that's happening. The chase is fun. I live for the chase, but there's always a point where it's easier to drop it and move on to someone else. Life has taught me that.

"Mr. Hughes, there's someone here to see you." Lance pokes his head around the corner, peering into my office. I need to start shutting the door.

"Who is it?" I bark back. I checked my calendar this morning. I've got nothing on tap today other than the early call I had with our office in Hong Kong. I've spent much of the day trying to wade through a stack of possible acquisitions. Nothing has caught my eye as of yet.

"It's a girl."

"You didn't get a name?" I study him and the grin on his face. What the fuck does Lance have going on in his life that keeps him this happy? I have to find out and whatever it is I need some of that too.

"I can go get one." He shrugs his shoulders. "I mean if you need a name."

"No, of course not," I try to say with as much sarcasm as I can possibly muster. I stand and pull my suit jacket back on. It's not unheard of for business associates to stop by unannounced. Women are an entirely different story. I rarely have a woman seek me out here. They know I draw a clear boundary around my work. Sex and business don't mesh in my world.

"I'll tell her to come in." He whips his head back around the doorjamb before he disappears out of sight.

I glance down at my phone when I see a text message coming in. It's Hunter, asking if I want to meet for a beer tonight. I tap out a short message telling him no. Tonight it's all about getting back in the saddle, which in my case is between the legs of a gorgeous woman.

"Alec. I mean, Mr. Hughes." Her voice stalls. "No, it's Alec. I'm sorry to bother you here but I was hoping we could talk."

That voice. It's breathy. It's soft. It's Libby. Libby Duncan is standing in the doorway of my office.

* * *

"I came here from rehearsal." She points at her outfit. "I should have gone home to change but I wanted to get this over with."

I want to get her over the arm of the leather couch we're now sitting on. She's wearing a white sweater, a small navy skirt and white kitten heels. I need to stop by rehearsal more often.

"We kissed when I was drunk." Her beautiful mouth thins. "I'm sorry. I mean I kissed you."

I lean back, resting my arm across the back of the couch. "I enjoyed it, Libby."

"Me too," she mutters beneath her breath. "I'm usually not like that."

Liar. I could tell from the way she was kissing me that Libby Duncan isn't a saint. "What are you usually like?"

Her eyes flit across my face before they land on the bank of windows that overlooks Wall Street. "I don't know. Not like that."

"I've heard it said that a person loses all their inhibitions when they're drinking." I tap my hand on my leg. "You wanted me that night."

Her breath stalls. She has to admit it. She can't possibly tell me that she wasn't as wet as she was. I felt it. I almost ripped those fucking panties off her body before I left. I should have. I'd still be carrying them around with me.

"I did want you." Her hand balls into a fist. "I don't want to though."

Now we're making progress. "Why don't you want to?"

"I moved here because I've always wanted to star on Broadway." She tilts her chin towards the windows. "It's really important to me. The musical, I mean. It's so important."

"I know it is."

"You own the play." Her gaze drops to her hands. "If we start this thing between us there's going to be a stigma attached to me."

She's right. I can't argue the point. People are going to know that Libby is the girl I'm fucking for this season. There are already mouths flapping at rehearsals when I show up. "I know your career is important to you." I mean it. I do know it. If it wasn't, she would have fucked me by now.

Her fingers rub the edge of her nose. "I've thought about things a lot."

Shit. Fuck it. This is when she tells me that her body is off limits because of Selfish Fate.

"If I wasn't in the musical, you wouldn't have wanted me." The words are direct and emotionless.

My eyes dart to hers. She's not looking for a response but there's no way in hell I'm going to allow her to carry that around with her. "That's not true."

"You saw me in the elevator that day and you knew I was in the play."

I did. I knew it before I got in the elevator. I saw her on the street and that's when I wanted her.

Her chest moves as she draws in a heavy breath. "Our attraction…" she stops with a small shake of her head. "Your attraction to me is based on the fact that I'm in the musical. I mean that's a big part of it, right?"

"No," I say firmly. "Libby, that's not it at all."

"You picked me because you knew you could offer me something." She pulls on the hem of her skirt. "I mean you thought you could offer me something in exchange for having sex with you."

"No." My voice is firm and controlled. "It's not about that, Libby. I am very attracted to you. Look at you. How could I not be? My desire to fuck you is about that. It's not about being able to offer you something in return."

"The other night when you took me for dinner, we almost fucked."

Christ, hearing that word come out of her mouth is making me hard. Timing is everything and right now mine sucks. I have to adjust myself on the couch just to hide the erection that is straining against my pants.

"I wanted to fuck you." Her tongue darts out of her mouth before she pulls it over her bottom lip. "I really did."

I shuffle in my seat. This can't be real. She's sitting inches away from me talking about wanting to feel my cock inside of her and I know she's about to get up and walk out of the door for good. I have to let her go. My mind is telling me it's the right thing to do, but my body is aching to get under that skirt. I had a taste of that on my fingers the other night, I need more.

"You don't want me now?" I ask knowing that the answer is either going to send my cock into overdrive or my erection will die a very quick and painful death.

She closes her eyes briefly before she opens them under heavy lids. "I didn't say that."

"Tell me what you want, Libby." I inch myself closer to her. "Tell me exactly what you want."

She arches her back as if she's looking for a place to retreat. She has nowhere to go but back into my lap. Her hands press down into the cushion on the couch. "I want this to be less complicated."

"Tell me how I can make that happen."

She wrings her hands together. I can feel the nervous energy bouncing off of her body. Her chest is heaving which is doing little to quell my raging hard-on. I want her naked, now. "I just want you to fuck me. That's all I want."

NINETEEN
LIBBY

I rehearsed what I wanted to say over and over again in my mind before I took the subway to Alec's office. I know he said that he could get me a solo in Selfish Fate but that would put a bull's eye on my back that says I'm being used. I don't want that. I just want the sex. He can keep the favors. I can make it on my own. I got the part in the musical from hard work and dedication. I'll climb up the rungs of the theatre world just like everyone else does.

"Did you just say you want me to fuck you, Libby?" His voice is a growl. It's different than it was ten minutes ago when I first stepped into his office and he slammed the door shut behind me.

My heart is racing. I didn't expect to be sitting so close to him when we had this conversation. I didn't expect to just blurt those words out either, but I have to own it now. "I said that, yes."

He lunges forward, pulling my body into his. His lips find mine in a hungry kiss and the only thing I can do is give in to the desperate want that I've been feeling for weeks. I moan into him as I cup the back of his head with my hand. His hair is soft and luxurious, his lips supple. He's such a good kisser. It's even better than I remember from when we kissed in his car the other night.

"Libby, you do things to me." The words press into my lips from his before his tongue pulls my mouth open.

I whimper when I feel his hand on my thigh. My body can't control its desperate need for him, so my legs fall open without thought. I'm so wet already. I was wet the moment I saw him through his office door.

His hand grazes my panties stopping over my clit. He presses his finger into it, through the fabric, causing a delicious bite of pressure with friction. I rock my hips with the motion. I'm hungry for this. I'm starving for his touch. I want to feel his hands on every part of me.

"I want you so much," he says hoarsely. "I can't stop thinking about you."

I close my eyes and give in to the kiss. I glide my lips over his, soaking in the taste of his breath. I need this too. I need to feel pleasure under this man's hands. I can pretend that I don't, but I want it. I can take it. I can have it and my part in the musical. I need to.

The moment he breaks the kiss, I feel bereft. I pop open my eyes. He's moving. He's lowering himself between my legs. I feel my panties being pulled down. My hand involuntarily falls into his hair.

"You have a beautiful body, Libby." He pulls his index finger through my moist slit. "I knew it would be perfect."

I arch my back to gain more of his touch. I want to feel his hands all over my body. "I want you to…"

He pushes my skirt up around my waist as he lowers his head to my core. He licks the entire length of my sex in one painfully slow movement. "I knew your cunt would be sweet."

His words pull everything that is within me to the surface. I cry out from the intensity of the pleasure. I moan every time his skilled tongue circles my clit and I reach for his hair with both hands when I feel his finger slide into me to touch my most sensitive spot.

"You're going to come for me, Libby." His words feather over my folds. "I want to watch your beautiful face as you come."

The words send me into an intense, delicious climax. I shudder from the depth of it. My lips part and a slow, involuntary moan trickles out. I hold fast to his hair, clinging to any part of him I can find. It's so much. It feels as though I'm going to burst apart from within.

I'm still floating in pleasure when he cups my ass in his palms, pulling my body into his mouth again. He's less tender this time, his tongue greedy and aggressive. He licks me hard, rakes his teeth over my clit and sucks it between his lips.

"Alec, please." I can barely form the words. "I feel so much."

"Take it, Libby," he growls into me. "Take it."

"God, yes." I moan into the silence.

I cry out from the intensity. I gaze down to see him still fully dressed in his suit, kneeling on the floor of his office with his head buried between my thighs. I grab the leather of the couch, close my eyes and let the second orgasm wash over me.

* * *

"Did I do something wrong?" I don't honestly know why I'm asking the question. All I did was come all over his face. I'm staring at him. The moist mist of my orgasm still lingers on his lips.

"Libby," he says my name quietly while he stares at me. "Libby, that was really nice."

You're telling me that was really nice? Excuse me, I'm the one who just had the two most intense orgasms I've ever had in my life.

"I liked it a lot," I offer because I'm a lame loser after I've come. My mind is a jumbled mess. I imagined he'd strip and fuck me hard right after he helped me climax, but that wasn't what happened at all. He'd leaned forward, kissed me tenderly and then he helped me put my panties back on.

"You should probably go." He stands now.

I don't cry after sex. Wait. I did cry once when the guy I was dating couldn't get me off. I cried because I was so frustrated. Right now, I feel something stirring within me. I can't say for certain that it's tears. All I know is that Alec Hughes ate me out and now he's throwing me out. I guess his mission was accomplished.

"You want me to go?" I ask for solid clarification. I'm still up for just about anything that includes his cock and mouth.

He scrubs his hand over the back of his neck. "I have work to do, Libby. You need to go."

Thank you for proving everyone in New York right, asshole. You are a pathetic man who only wants to fuck women. In my case, I don't even rate for a fuck. I just got a pussy eating. What does that earn me? A new watch? Maybe a fast food meal? Fuck, I am an idiot.

"I can have Gabriel drive you home." He moves towards the phone on his desk.

I jump to my feet, smoothing my skirt and adjusting my sweater. "No. I'll take the subway."

"It's just as fast for Gabriel to take you."

I guess I have my answer. My payment for our brief, but admittedly satisfying romp, on the couch is a ride in his fancy car. "I'm going to take the subway."

"Libby," he says my name as he starts back towards me. "I'm glad you came to my office today."

Are you now? I should say something. I should tell him what a jerk he is. I should let him know exactly what I'm feeling but it's just a waste of time. I heard the stories. I knew about him. It's my own fault that I didn't listen to the whispered warnings about him.

"I better go." I turn and without looking back I walk out of his office.

TWENTY

ALEC

We all have defining moments in our lives. For some people it's when they graduate from college. Other people claim it's the day they got married, while there's some who will tell you that it's the day their child was born. My defining moment was today. It was an hour ago when I let Libby Duncan walk out of my office. I didn't exactly let her walk out. If I'm being honest with myself I practically pushed her plump, perfect ass right out the door. Jesus, fucking Christ I am an idiot.

"Mr. Hughes, do you need anything before I leave?" Lance is back. Goddamn Lance is back in the doorway of my office chirping about doing something for me. Maybe he can tell me why I acted like the biggest bastard on the planet after I ate Libby Duncan to orgasm. Maybe he can tell me why I didn't whip my cock out and fuck her senseless.

"I need a redo of the last two hours of my life," I say through clenched teeth.

"Did something happen with that girl?" he whispers before stepping through my office door and slamming it shut.

I look past him to the door. "Did I ask you to come in here?"

"She looked pretty upset when she stormed out of your office." He crosses his arms over his chest. "Is she your girlfriend? I mean I know what people say about you and women."

"What the fuck do people say about me and women?" That was purely a reflexive response. I don't need Lance to spell it out for me. I've got a pretty good handle on my own reputation.

He rubs his hand over his forehead. "Let's just say you do well with the ladies."

Let's just say you're fired and call it a day. "Libby is different."

"Was that Libby?" He circles around with his hand flying towards the door. "That's Libby Duncan?"

"That's her." I raise both brows. "That's Jensen Duncan's daughter."

"She looks nothing like I expected."

"What the hell does that mean?" I push my chair away from my desk. I desperately need a drink. I've got to get to a bar now.

"I pictured her differently in my mind. I thought she'd be taller and brunette. I also thought she'd…"

"Who the fuck cares what you thought?" I'm paying his salary. He knows it. I know it. I'm allowed an occasional outburst.

It doesn't faze him in the least. "What happened, sir? My friends come to me for relationship advice. I'm kind of a guru if I'm being honest. I can help."

All of that bullshit didn't just come from his mouth, did it? Did I seriously just hear that? "What the fuck, Lance? I'm not talking to you about Libby."

"It would help," he says the words with conviction.

"You're not my therapist." I tuck my smartphone into the pocket of my pants. "You're not going to be my assistant anymore either unless you get out of here now and get back to work."

"It's after six."

"So?" I toss the question out as I brush past him towards my office door.

"I'm done for the day, sir."

"I'm done for the day too. I can't wait for this fucking day to be over."

* * *

"Wait a minute." She places her hand on my knee as she teeters on the very edge of the stool next to the bar. "You're telling me that there are two different kinds of sex?"

No, this is not a repeat of the Lucy clusterfuck. I'm not about to run back into a hotel room with just any woman. I should. I should be watching a woman blow me right now, but I'm not.

"There is a hell of a lot more kinds of sex than just two, sweetheart."

"Oh, I know." The words flow from her with a purr. Judging by the way this redhead is grabbing my knee, no, wait, my thigh, she's not afraid to try anything.

"I'm talking about sex with feelings and sex just for the sake of fucking."

She takes another swallow of the apple martini I bought her when she first sat down. "So you ate her out and then what? You fell in love with her?"

"I'm not in love with her." I tilt the glass of bourbon in my hand, watching the remainder of the amber liquid pool to one side. "That's not what I mean."

"Explain it then." She leans forward on the bar. "I've never understood the guys I've fucked. I'd like to hear this."

"She came twice." I hold up two fingers. "I was so ready to fuck her. I wanted to. Christ, I wanted to."

"Why didn't you?"

"I fuck a lot of women." I'm not proud of it. I've never been proud of it. It feels an empty void inside of me. I recognize that. I may not admit it to anyone, but I'm smart enough to see it. "I don't feel shit for any of them, but she's different."

"How so?" She motions for the bartender to bring her another drink.

I hold up my now empty glass at wave it at him. "I could have licked her pussy for hours. Jesus, it was sweet. Those fucking soft sounds she was making. The way her ass wiggled in my hands. It was amazing."

"You're making me want that." She squirms on the stool, her hand inching up my thigh.

I stare at it. It's doing nothing for me. She's about ready to grab my balls through my pants and I'm not feeling it at all. All I want to do is talk about Libby. "You're not getting it from me."

Her hand squeezes my thigh even tighter. "The night is still young."

I ignore the comment. The last thing I want right now is to wash away the taste of Libby with another woman. That's not happening. "I can't stop thinking about her."

"If that's true, it makes no sense that you didn't fuck her when you had the chance."

She's right. I didn't fuck Libby when I had the chance. She was all splayed out on the couch in my office, her skirt hiked up to her waist, her beautiful pussy on full display and I dressed her and threw her out.

"You may have your own theory about this, but do you want to know what I think?" She downs half the martini the bartender just put in front of her.

"I'm dying to hear this." I take a sip of the bourbon, sliding a piece of ice between my lips.

"You knew that if you fucked her, it would change the way you feel about her."

"How would it do that?"

"You said she's different right?" She raises the glass in the air.

I nod. "She's very different."

"Maybe fucking her would make her just like the rest of them." She tugs at the bottom of her dress, which is rider higher and higher with each movement she makes.

I glance briefly at her legs. "You're suggesting that if I fucked her, I'd view her in the same way as every other woman I've fucked?"

"I know men like you." She pulls her hand away from my thigh and rests it on the bar. "You fuck a woman once or twice and then you walk away. You don't look back. You probably even give them parting gifts."

This nameless redhead has me all figured out. "I've done that in the past, yes."

She raises a brow to challenge me. "It's your thing. I can tell."

"You can tell?" Have I fucked this woman? I'm beginning to feel like she knows me better than I know myself.

She shifts in her seat. "I've seen you in here before. I've seen you leave with different woman. I've never seen you walk out of here with the same woman twice."

I've been that obvious? Christ, I've been a fucking asshole. Maybe she's right. Maybe I don't want Libby to become one of the random women I've fucked, and then forgotten.

Her eyes dart behind me. "I see someone I know over there. We're not going to fuck, right?"

"No. We're not going to fuck."

"Your loss." She slides off the bar stool, her hand darting to my shoulder. "Don't fuck it up with her, Charlie. You might not get a second chance with a girl like that."

She's right. I need to fix things with Libby now.

TWENTY ONE
LIBBY

"Sometimes I think about moving back to Denver." I cover my mouth to stifle a heavy yawn. "I miss it."

"You miss how boring your life was?" Claudia taps her hand on the table. "You don't miss it there, Lib. You just get all sentimental when things aren't going your way."

I can't argue that point. I've done the same thing every few months since I've been in New York. It happened each time I was passed over for a role. It happened when the first guy I dated here told me he wasn't into me and it's happening now. This time it's Alec's fault. He's the one who told me he wanted to fuck me and then when I gave myself to him, he rejected me. The bitter sting of that is still there, even though it's been more than a week since I was in his office with him.

"What happened this time?"

I should tell her. I should confess it all to her. Claudia can keep a secret. It's not as though she's going to rush up to Alec and tell him I was talking about him. She wouldn't do that. Would she?

"Have you ever been with a guy who really wanted you and then when you gave yourself to him he rejected you?" That sounds so completely pathetic. I should have rehearsed this when I was in the shower this morning. Hearing the words now I realize I don't need her opinion at all. I need to stay away from Alec Hughes.

"Like during sex? Did some guy reject you during sex, Lib?"

I've just opened a can of worms and I'm never going to be able to close it back up again. "No, it's not me. It's a friend."

"What friend?" she spits out.

How can I blame her? I have a handful of friends in this city. She practically knows every single one of them. "It's no one you know. It's someone from back home."

"Oh," she says with a confused look on her face. "Guys are crazy. Tell your friend to find a different guy who appreciates her."

It's good, solid advice. "Did you hear anything more about the auditions for the touring company of Falling Choices?"

"They're going to be next month." She doesn't take her eyes off her smartphone. "They're hand picking people to audition. Do you know anyone who can get us in?"

As much as my dreams have always involved getting a lead part in a Broadway play, landing a major role in the touring company of Falling Choices is the next best thing. I'd seen the production at least a dozen times. I can sing every song from the show and I'm at the point now where I can almost literally recite the entire book line-for-line. It's my favorite musical of all time and if given the chance, I'd put my Broadway aspirations on hold to go on tour with that company.

"Maybe I can talk to Sharma?" I feel deflated by the news that it's not an open audition. "Maybe she has some pull. I really want this. I think I could land a lead role."

"I want you to get a part in that, Lib." She stands up in one fluid movement and juts her hand towards me. "Get up. Our break is over. It's time to get back in there."

She's right. I need to get my head back into Selfish Fate. For now, it's my ticket to a career on Broadway so I need to stay focused and on track. With Alec Hughes out of my life there's nothing that will get in my way.

* * *

I see the car the moment I round the corner. I don't want my heart to react this way. I don't want my body to betray me the way it is. Why the hell am I getting so excited by the knowledge that Alec Hughes is waiting in front of my apartment building for me? He treated me like a throw-away the other day and now my pulse is racing knowing I'm going to be looking at his beautiful green eyes any second.

I up my pace when I see Gabriel exit the car and walk around it. I don't look in his direction when I see the shadow of his large frame step out of the back seat and I don't react at all when I hear him say my name.

I try to walk past him but the street is filled with people. I'm not more than ten paces away from my front door and I'm trapped. Alec is standing directly in front of me.

"Libby, please." His hand is on my shoulder. "Look at me."

I can't. I know what I'm feeling. I'm hurt. I'm angry, but more than anything, I'm humiliated.

"I don't know why you're here." I direct my words to the ground, my eyes focused on a small piece of grass fighting its way through a crack in the concrete. "I don't want to see you."

He exhales. The rush of air from his mouth skims my cheek. "Libby." He's so close to me now. He's bent forward. He's trying to get me to make eye contact with him but I can't.

"I need to get upstairs." I take a step to the left but he mirrors my action.

"Let me come up."

I can't. I want to. The part of me that is pathetic and weak wants him to come up. That part wants him to slide his tongue over my clit again. It wants him to strip naked so I can drop to my knees and take him in my mouth. It's the part that dreams of having his cock inside of me, pounding it into me until I have the most explosive orgasm I've ever had. That's the part of me I need to tie up so it doesn't get in the way.

I finally lift my eyes to his face. Christ, Libby. Why the fuck would you do that? You know he's too beautiful for words. You know women can't resist him and you're a woman so what the hell were you thinking?

"I'm busy, Alec," I try to say the words through dry lips. "I don't think we have anything to talk about."

"I'm just asking for a few minutes." His voice is different. It's not bold and confident. It's cracking. There's vulnerability in it that I haven't heard before.

I know I shouldn't do this. I know that I need to tell him to fuck off and leave me alone but my mouth says the two words that my heart needs it to. "Come inside."

TWENTY TWO

ALEC

"I was such a fucking asshole in my office, Libby," I spit the words out in haste the moment she closes the door. I can't honestly believe she agreed to let me up. Now that I'm standing here I have no idea how to fix this mess I've made.

She places her bag down and turns to look at me. "Is that an apology?"

An apology? Jesus. I should be giving her that and more. "I'm sorry, Libby. I'm sorry for the way I treated you."

"Why are you here?" She kicks her heels off. "How long were you waiting out there?"

If I'm going to be honest I've been tracking her movements all day. I stood in the corner of the rehearsal hall watching her dance and sing hours ago. After that I peered through the window of the jewelry store watching her sell a necklace to an older man. I was mesmerized by the smile on her face as she patiently showed him one necklace after another until he finally chose the one he purchased. Once she was off work, I had Gabriel bring me here.

"You've apologized, Alec. You can leave." She starts towards the door.

I move a step to the left to block her path. I know that she can easily dart around me but I also know that she won't. If she didn't want to hear me out, she wouldn't have let me in. "I have some things I want to say."

"So say them." She rests her hands on her hips. "I'm all ears."

"Can I sit down?" I need to relax. I need to calm the fuck down if I'm going to do this correctly.

She sweeps her hands towards that lumpy as hell couch of hers. "Be my guest."

I sit, trying to position my weight so any wayward springs don't find their way up my ass. "I don't usually act like that after I go down on a woman." Why does that sound completely offensive?

There's absolutely no hiding the disgust in her expression. "This isn't helping."

"Libby." I lean forward, as much to curb the distance between us as to keep my cock in one piece. This fucking couch is a death trap. "What we did in my office was intense for me."

She taps her hand on the arm of the chair she's sitting in. "Intense in what way?"

Not exactly the response I thought I'd get but I can work with it. "I don't usually care about the women I have sex with. Tasting you was amazing. It made me feel things."

"What things?" Her hand traces a path along the fabric of the chair, her eyes following it.

"I was overwhelmed with how good it felt. I didn't want you to just be another woman that I fucked, Libby." I strain to control my breathing. It's rapid and uneven. I'm confessing things aloud I've never felt before in my life. "I had to stop and think. I was a dick for the way I handled it."

I watch her intently. I see the small smile that overtakes her beautiful mouth. I see the way her hand relaxes on the chair. I need to keep this moving forward if I expect her to give me another chance.

"I'd like us to spend more time together."

Her gaze moves up until she's staring directly at me. "As in the arrangement you talked about?"

I scratch the back of my head. I feel so completely uncomfortable. I haven't talked about my feelings in years. Most of the time, I forget I even have feelings. "No, I want this to be different."

"What do you mean? Different in what way?"

"I know you have concerns about your work." I pat the edge of her knee. "I know how important your role in the musical is to you."

She nods slightly. "I worked really hard to get it."

I'm sure she did. I had no say in casting choices until Sharma summoned me down to the rehearsal hall that morning I first saw Libby. "I have no doubt about that. I don't want to jeopardize that for you."

Her shoulders lean forward. I recognize the relief in them. "My job is the most important thing in the world to me."

You wouldn't expect to hear those words coming from a young woman who is set to inherit a billion dollar corporation one day. It's something we have in common, even if she's not aware of it. I never sat back and enjoyed the spoils of my father's hard work either. I got my ass into college, got a degree and worked my way up in our company. Libby is doing the very same thing. The only difference is that she had the guts to chase her own dreams. She's got the education to back up her father's investments, but she's making a life on her own. I respect her for that.

"I know you said you'd get me a solo at one point," she begins before she stops to take in a breath. "I don't want that. I want to make it on my own. I need to prove it to myself."

"I know that you do," I offer softly. "I'm amazed by your talent."

"You've never heard me sing." Her face lights up in a wide smile. "You don't know if I'm talented or not."

I lean back again doing my best to avoid the mine field that is the springs in her couch. "I've been at rehearsals. I've watched you sing and dance. The stage is where you belong."

"You've been there?"

"A few times." I reach to rest my arm on the back of the sofa.

She lifts her chin slightly, tilting forward in her seat. "You're full of surprises."

"You have no idea. You have no fucking idea." I close my eyes to ward off the always present memories of my fucked up past. I need to start looking at my future and now is as good a time as any. "Have dinner with me tomorrow, Libby. Let's try this again."

TWENTY THREE

LIBBY

"What are the rules?" I feel nervous energy bouncing throughout my entire body. Alec Hughes just asked me out. I want this. I mean I think I want this. I wouldn't even be considering it if he hadn't apologized for what happened in his office.

"Rules?" He's on his feet, smoothing the hem of his suit jacket. "What do you mean?"

I'm confused and I'm sure my expression isn't hiding that at all. "You don't just go on dates with women without rules in place, do you?"

He buttons the jacket stopping to remove a stray piece of lint. "I guess I don't. I haven't actually gone on a lot of dates the past few years."

"Can I ask you something about that?" I lean in closer as if the walls can hear me. "I mean if it's okay to talk about it."

"Talk about what?" His jaw clenches. "What are you asking me about?"

"When you sleep with women, do they always take the gifts you offer to them?" It's been there, right on the edge of my lips waiting for me to ask it. I've never been around a man who treated sex like a business arrangement before.

He takes a step back. I can tell I've offended him. "I treat women well, Libby. I think you've jumped to some incorrect conclusions about me."

"I'm sorry if it sounded as though I was judging you." I want that to sound completely genuine, because it is. We all make our own choices. I'm just trying to understand him more.

He rubs his temple with his left hand. "My life is very busy so I seek out women who are looking for the same thing I am."

"I understand," I say under my breath. I don't really understand. I just want to understand how it impacts my time with him.

"I'm a generous person. If a woman I'm interested in needs something and I have the ability to give it to her, I want to."

I stare at his face. It's stoic and emotionless. "I was just curious."

"Libby," he whispers my name quietly into the still air between us. "I don't want you to think so much about this. I want you to enjoy it. We're just two people who are going to go on a date or two."

A date or two? He's right. I'm asking about his moral compass and he just asked me out to dinner. I need to slow things down. "You're right."

"You're not working at the jewelry store tomorrow night, are you?"

"Not tomorrow, no."

He adjusts one of his cufflinks, pulling the sleeve of his dress shirt in line with his jacket. "I'll be here for you at eight."

I follow him to the door, stopping when he turns to look at me. "I'm looking forward to it."

"Me too," he whispers softly against my lips. "I'll see you tomorrow."

* * *

"This view must be amazing." I stare out the large window towards Central Park.

I hear him behind me before his hand touches my elbow. "When you come back during the day, you'll see for yourself."

I turn to look at him, taking the wine glass that he's holding out for me. I need to pay attention to how much I'm drinking tonight. I don't want a repeat of what happened after we left Axel NY. "I didn't realize we'd be having dinner at your place."

"It's not," he begins before he takes a sip of the wine. "It's not always comfortable going to a restaurant. Sometimes I prefer ordering in."

"If I lived here, I'd never go out." I dip my head. My gaze stops on the simple black dress I'm wearing. I feel so misplaced in such a beautiful space. "This is such a nice condo."

His eyes dart over my face. "I've wanted to ask you something, Libby."

I need reinforcement before I hear this so I take a healthy swallow of the wine. That's all I'll have. It's going to be enough to take the edge off without throwing me into his lap again. "What is it?"

"I know who your father is." His jaw tightens. "I've been wondering why you live in that apartment."

I sigh. It shouldn't surprise me that he's jumped to the assumption that my father is footing the bill for my adventures in New York City. My entire life it's been the same story.

I come from money therefore I should have money. "It's all I can afford."

A sly smirk rakes over his mouth. "I know how much your father is worth, Libby. You can afford better."

I push my head back, stretching my neck, trying to rid myself of the tension I feel taking over my shoulders. It's a conversation that was inevitable. I know that people like Alec find it necessary to run background checks on those they spend time with. My father's done the same thing. "My father can afford better. I can't."

"You've lost me. What are you trying to say?"

I try not to smile. It's a foreign concept to him because he's rich. He's grown up with money, just as I did. The difference is that his father gave him the reins of the family business and set him on his own course. "My father doesn't pay my way."

I can see the surprise in his expression although he's trying to mask it by taking another healthy swallow from his glass. "You're surviving in this city on your wage from the musical?"

Irony is rarely a welcome guest. He's questioning how I'm living on the paltry wage he's giving me. "No. That's why I work at the jewelry store. I'm paid in commissions there."

"You have a degree, Libby."

They are a repeat of the words my father said before I left. I'd worked hard for my degree. I finished early and was hungry for the chance to jump into a position within my father's company. "I'm proud of it," I offer.

"Do you plan on using it one day? Are you going to take over your father's business?"

I can't say I'm surprised by the question. It's Alec's life path. I know his history. I know that he's built his father's empire up to what it is today. It's a conglomerate that many in the business world envy. Their vast array of holdings includes everything from Fortune 500 companies to burgeoning start-ups. Alec Hughes is a genius when it comes to business. It's no wonder he'd expect me to be using my degree to chase the same dream he is.

"Am I asking too many questions?" His hand lightly taps my shoulder. "Is this something you'd rather not talk about?"

Avoidance can be a good thing, but in this case it's only prolonging the unavoidable. I sense that if I don't tell Alec how I ended up as a glorified extra in his musical that he'll send someone out to hunt down the information. He may as well hear it from me. "We can talk about it."

"Over dinner." He gestures towards a dining table. "You can explain everything to me."

TWENTY FOUR
ALEC

I'll never understand men like Jensen Duncan. They have a brilliant, bright, eager daughter and they pass her over for a lazy son who has absolutely no ambition. I can't complain about it too much. Her father's reluctance to give her a position of power brought Libby to New York City. Now, she's sitting in my condo eating dinner. I should thank her father for that.

"Have you lived here long?" She places the fork down on the edge of the plate before she pulls the linen napkin across her lips.

I need to answer that. This is where the lies start. "A few years."

"It's a nice area of the city." She picks up the wine glass, studies it and then sets it back down without bringing it to her mouth.

"It is," I offer back. Christ, why is one little lie tearing me up inside? "Do you like where you live?"

"You don't like where I live." Her eyes brighten. "I can tell when you're there."

"It's not that I don't like the place." I push my plate aside. "I don't like that fucking couch you always tell me to sit on."

"What's wrong with it?" she asks sweetly.

It's the actress part of her again. It has to be. That wide grin on her face isn't hiding a thing.

"It's fucking deadly, Libby. The springs in that thing are determined to take off my left nut." I reach down and graze my hand across my crotch. "Next time I'm standing."

"You're exaggerating." She runs her hand lightly across her cheek. "It's not that bad."

I want to tell her that I'll give her a raise so she can move to a different place. Hell, I want to set her up in a new place tonight. I can't stand the thought of her going back there. It's not where she belongs. She's way too good for it. She's way too good for me.

"I'm glad I agreed to have dinner with you."

I hate when she does that. I hate when she's sweet and so fucking genuine. I don't want her to be polite. I don't need her to make me feel things. I just want her to use me, the way women have been using me for years.

"Come with me Libby." I stand and reach out my hand to her in one easy movement. "There's something I want to show you."

* * *

"This is an actual Tony award, Alec."

I look down into her face. She's glowing. She's cradling the statue in her hands, her eyes running over it, taking in every nuance and circular curve. "It is an actual Tony."

She sighs softly as she hands it back to me. "Where did you get it?"

I pull my brow into a mock scowl. "I've backed a few plays in the past few years, Libby."

"Not one of them ever received a nomination."

I laugh before placing it back down on the desk in my home office. "How do you know that?"

She giggles causing the hair that is resting on her shoulders to fall forward. There's something wildly innocent about her but at the same time she's one of the most provocative women I've ever been around. She's the perfect balance of softness and seductive all wrapped up in a tight body and flawless face.

I push her hair back into place. "The award was a gift." I don't elaborate. I should. I should tell her that I bought it at an auction to give to someone.

"That's a really nice gift." She runs her hand along the base. "The person who gave it to you must have cared about you a lot."

It's a question wrapped up in a statement. It's not one I can answer though. I need to leave her assumption as it. "It's been a good source of inspiration. I hope Selfish Fate gets a few nominations this year."

"I do too."

"You look so happy when you're rehearsing." I take a step closer to her. "You're in your element when you're singing and dancing."

She bows her head slightly as the faint light in the room catches her earrings. "I feel best when I'm performing. I feel like me."

"I can tell," I whisper the words softly into the stillness of the room.

I want to touch her. Christ, I seriously want to touch her. It's taken all the self-control I have not to lunge at her and pull her into the bedroom. I can't push her though. She's not like the others. I want her to want me.

She turns so she's facing me directly now. Her eyes lock with mine. "I don't want anyone from work to know that I came here."

I'm playing with fire. I'm so fucking deep right now that I can't think straight. I need to take her home. I need to walk as far away from her as I can and let her live her life. I need to tell her to chase that goddamn neighbor of hers she said she was hot for. I need this to stop. I can't let this stop. "No one will know you were here."

"You promise?" she asks, her eyes close slightly. "No one will know about us?"

"I don't advertise what I do in my private life." My hand sweeps over her chin. "If you want to keep this quiet, I'm make that happen."

Her beautiful brown eyes lock with mine. "Make it happen."

I take the words literally. I pull her supple body into mine, sweep my lips over hers and give in to my unending need for Libby Duncan.

TWENTY FIVE
LIBBY

"Christ, Libby, please." His hands tangle wildly in my hair, the pressure soft enough to show the tenderness I need, yet aggressive enough to express that even when he's in the most vulnerable of positions, he's still the one in control.

My lips splay over the wide head. I suck on it gently, knowing he needs time to adjust to the pressure of my mouth. He's large, he's thick, and he's beautiful. I'd imagined his cock since I saw him in the elevator. I'd anticipated its taste since he pushed himself against me and its outline on my stomach held the promise of a depth of pleasure I'd never known before.

After he told me he'd keep things quiet, I'd fallen to my knees. The act itself was out of sheer need. I want to taste him. I need to please him. I have to give him what he gave to me.

"Lick it." His voice is hoarse and rich.

I acquiesce, wanting him to direct me to the rush he's seeking. I look up. His head is thrown back. One of his hands moves behind him to the window sill, gripping the wooden frame. His legs part slightly. He's still fully dressed. I'd fumbled briefly with his fly, before he'd taken over, pulling it open, pushing his boxer briefs down and releasing his swollen cock for me.

I run my tongue along the length of it, marveling in the hardness of the dense root. I moan as it jumps slightly under my touch. It's mine right now. This is the moment I've longed for.

"Fuck, you have a sweet mouth."

His words are shameless. They're heady and hot and spur me on. I twist my tongue around him, lashing the head again and again with soft gentle strokes. I suck harder now, wanting him to find a rhythm.

"Ah, fuck, Libby, fuck." His hips move, faster and harder with each thrust. His hands leap back into my hair, cupping my head, using it for leverage as he fucks my mouth with long, even strokes.

I grip his legs. My hands hold tight to his strong, muscular thighs as he takes everything I'm giving to him.

"This is so good. It's too good." He pumps harder.

I suck him with no inhibition, taking more of him into my throat with each thrust of his hips. I moan from the sensation. I groan from the desperate need to taste everything he's going to give to me. It's so much yet it's still not enough.

"I'm going to fucking come," he hisses into the darkness. "Swallow it, Libby. Take it all."

I dig my knees into the floor, open my mouth wider and take every drop he offers me.

* * *

"Take your clothes off," he whispers the words into my lips. We're in his bedroom now, my arms around his neck. The intimate kiss we're sharing broken only by his need to have more.

I pull at my dress, freeing it from my body. His hands take over, undoing the front clasp of my bra before his head dips down to claim my nipple in his mouth. He pulls at it, wetting it with his tongue. It hardens instantly, the ache within it a desperate yearning that is now coursing hot through every part of me.

My hands drop to my panties. I dip my hand inside. I have to come. The taste of his desire still lingers on my tongue. He offered so much. I'd struggled to take it all. His eyes had widened when he saw it falling from around his cock, seeping out of my lips. I'd lapped it all up. I was greedy. I was unashamed. I was hungry for him.

"I need to fuck you," he says it out loud first but it's just a mirrored reflection of the ache within me. I need him to fuck me too. I need to feel his cock inside of me, giving me what I've craved for weeks.

I lean back, hooking my hands in thin fabric of my panties. I pull them down in one movement. I want him to see me. I want him to see how his hands and lips have pulled my desire right to the surface.

He strips quickly. His cock bobbing heavy and hard in the air as he walks to a dresser, reaching inside to pull out a condom. He rips the package open, tearing the foil in his teeth, dropping the remnants on the floor. He sheaths his cock swiftly, his eyes never leaving my face.

I stare at his strong, powerful body as he lifts me and pushes me back onto the bed. I taste his lips as he runs the wide head of his erection over my sex. I nod my head when he asks if I can take it all and then I scream from the bite of pain as he enters me fully.

I cry out his name as I fly over the edge into an almost instant orgasm. The brush of his thumb over my clit as he fucks me slowly is enough to push me, but the foreplay has been teasing me for weeks. Each touch of his hand against me, each word of lust that he's spoken to me, his head between my legs stealing my pleasure from me in his office. It's all been there, just at the surface, pushing me into this place I am now.

"Alec," I call his name into his shoulder. "Oh God."

He pumps himself into me, stalling as I savor my release. His hands cup my cheeks. His tongue traces my bottom lip as I settle back down into his rhythm.

"You're cunt is so tight, Libby. It's so fucking tight."

The words are blunt, direct and fall from his mouth into the flesh of my neck. The moist mist on his skin slides into mine. He pulls my legs around his waist, burying himself deeper in me.

My name tumbles from his lips and breezes against my cheek. His cock grows inside of me stretching me more. He takes my body with long, graceful strokes pulling me towards the edge again.

"Come again, Libby." The words are soft and break through the barrier of pleasure I'm feeling. "I need you to come."

I fly into the throes of an intense orgasm, clinging tightly to him does little to quell my body's reaction. I flail beneath him, my hips rocking, my legs jerking, my body shuddering as he rallies back, calls out my name and fucks me hard until he finally gives me everything he has.

TWENTY SIX

ALEC

What the fuck was that? That wasn't like anything I've felt before.

It's late. It's after midnight. I'd cradled Libby in my arms afterwards. I did it as much for myself as for her. Helping her dress, driving her home and walking her to her door had been hell. This is where I usually end it. This is when I delete a woman's number and call it a fucking day.

I can't.

I won't.

Not this time.

Fucking Libby Duncan made every woman I'd ever been with wash out of my memory. I can't remember anything but the curves of her hips and the scent of her skin. She is all that I want.

I finish my glass of brandy as I stare out in the darkness of the city that I love. New York is my home. It's the place I belong. I grew up here, learned about life here. I've met some of the best friends I have here and more women than I can count. The foundation of my life is here even though my parents moved to Greece years ago. Everything I love is here, along with everything I loathe.

I walk to the bedroom, turn on the overhead light and curse inwardly at the glare as it hits my eyes. I want to get in that bed. I want to smell her skin again. I want to remember what it felt like to feel myself inside of her when she came, my name a breathless whisper on her lips.

I walk to the bed, run my hand along the imprint that her body made when she laid next to me to catch her breath. I want her back here. I need her back in this bed with her legs wrapped around me while I bury myself in her cunt, feeling her milking everything I have.

I slam the empty glass down with a dull, vacant thud onto the dresser. I switch off the lights before rounding the corner to the main room. I pick up my suit jacket, slide it back over my shoulders, take one last look around and walk out the door.

I slide my finger over the screen of my smartphone before stabbing the elevator call button. "Hey, Jasmine." I swallow past the lump in my throat. "I'm on my way home. I'll be there in fifteen."

* * *

"We've made some significant changes to the book." Sharma points to the binder she placed in front of me when she arrived at my office ten minutes ago. "You should read it over."

I should throw it in the trash. Unless the musical has an entirely new storyline this thing is still going to hit the ground crawling. I'm investing more and more money in it with the full knowledge that it's going to run through previews and then close. It's a hot mess and not in any way is that a good thing.

"I've been to some of the rehearsals," I say trying to think of how to approach this diplomatically. "The musical is a piece of shit." Softening the blow isn't going to change that fact.

Her eyes widen. I can't tell if she's stunned because I've offended her or if I've confirmed exactly what she's thinking. "It's a work in progress."

"It's opening soon." I point out. "Any progress you're making needs to happen today."

She grips the handle of the chair she's sitting in. "We've added a solo for one of the chorus girls, as you requested."

"Shit," I mumble under my breath. I'd asked for that shortly after meeting Libby when we were volleying the idea of her getting a solo back and forth. What the fuck am I supposed to do now? She's made it crystal clear that she wants nothing from me in exchange for our time together.

"What did you say?"

She knows exactly what I said. "We may need to remove that."

"We're not removing it." Her hand taps the top of the binder. "We worked for days to add that, Mr. Hughes. An entire scene had to be rewritten to accommodate that. If we change it now, it's going to delay opening night. We'll have to push back previews. It's going to cost you a lot more."

Thanks a hell of a lot for pointing out that I'm footing this exercise in inevitable failure, Sharma. I stare at her across from my desk. This is my problem now. It's not hers. I need to talk to Libby about the solo. It's hers if she wants it but I know she'll refuse.

"What do you think?" she presses. "Do you want it changed again?"

"Fuck." I spit out. "Fuck, no. Leave it as is."

"Do you have someone in mind for the solo or should I be holding auditions?"

Libby's words race through my mind. She doesn't want to be singled out. "Do the auditions."

"Good." Her nostrils fume. "There's another matter we need to discuss."

This shit is never ending. I have actual, moneymaking business to get to. I need for this meeting to be over. "What?"

"It's Libby Duncan."

My eyes shoot up to rest on hers. "What about her?"

"She asked me for a favor." She nervously taps the edge of her knee. "I thought you'd want to know."

I'm not one to pass by an opportunity to do some damage control. "What does that have to do with me? You're her boss. You should be handling favors."

She raises both brows. "I just thought you'd want to know."

"Does it involve the show?" That's a fucked up question. Why wouldn't it be about the show? I need to calm the fuck down when Libby's name is mentioned.

"She has a contract with us and she's been asking about getting out of it."

What. The. Fuck.

I scrub my hand over the back of my neck. Libby wants to quit the show? That has to be because of what happened between us. "She asked you about getting out of her contract?"

"Not point blank or anything." She crosses one leg over the other. "She wants me to put in a good word with a friend who is handling the auditions for another show."

"What show?"

"It's for Falling Choices. They're going to hold auditions for the touring company. I actually think Libby has a good chance of getting a lead." For good measure she adds," I have a friend there I can talk to about getting her in."

"No," I say without thinking. "I'll handle it."

I will handle it. This audition can change everything. There's no way in hell I'm letting anyone deal with this but me.

TWENTY SEVEN

LIBBY

"You think you can ignore me and I won't hunt you down."

The words echo through my body. I don't turn around. I don't need to. I know his voice. I know the low grumble that's woven into the syllable of the words. I know the sound of his need as it leaves his lips. I heard it when he took me to his condo on Central Park West and fucked me three nights ago.

"You said you'd keep it private." I push my lips to my shoulder, directing the words back at him. "This is public. You need to leave."

His response is a hand on my hip. He thrusts his body into me, his cock angling between the cheeks of my ass. It's covered in a dress so thin that he can feel every contour and curve. "You want to be fucked."

"You fucked me already," I whimper the words without the intention. My body instinctively reacts to his voice, his touch and the promise of being taken by him again.

His breath is hot on my neck. "I want to fuck you again, Libby."

"You can't be here." I press my hands flat against the display case. "I'm working."

He pulls on the hem of my dress. "I'm going to slide my fingers into your tight, wet cunt right here and right now."

I lunge forward, not as much from the promise of the words but the ache in my sex. "No, Alec. We can't."

His hand inches higher and I fall back into him from the burden of my desire. It's there. It's always there, pulling me down. It's a weight within me that can't be satiated by my own hand. I've tried in desperation for days to find the same pleasure that he found. I've rubbed my fingers through my folds while I've been in bed at night, imagining his glorious tongue racing over my pussy. I've pushed two fingers into my channel hoping to capture the intensity that was there when he slid his cock into me, stretching me to my limits. It was futile and frustrating. I need what only he can give me.

"Lock the door, Libby." His fingers fly past my face towards a large clock on the wall. "It's eight. The store is closed."

I move quickly, pulling the deadbolt into place. I turn off the overhead lights so curious shoppers won't peek in hoping to get a glimpse of the beautiful creations that the store is known for.

He's there the instant I twist around, his lips on mine. I moan into the kiss as he thrusts his lush tongue into my mouth.

"I can't stop this, Libby." His hands are under my dress, seeking my core.

I push my legs apart, wanting desperately to feel any touch he's offering to me. "Don't stop."

He rips my panties from me in one fierce movement. His hand covers my sex pressing into it. The pressure is enough to bring me to my knees, but he holds steadfast to my body, pushing me into the wall. "I've thought about your greedy cunt for days, Libby."

"No." The words speak of a need I don't want to have. It's there. I feel it and he sees it, but it's too much.

"No?" His lips run over my cheek. "No, your cunt isn't hungry for me?"

I shake my head, not wanting to give voice to the words. I reach for his pants, wanting to free his cock. He wants me just as much as I want him. I'm going to prove it to him.

"When I was buried inside your body, Libby," he begins as his hands latch onto mine pulling them into his chest. "You were stroking me from within. You were so wet, so needy. You were clenching me, pulling out everything I had to give to you."

"Stop," I whisper with no conviction. "I'm not like that."

"What are you like?" His voice is a growl from deep within. "You've been thinking about me since I took you home."

I breathe in the scent of his skin. It's strong and male. The cologne he wears is intoxicating. "I thought about you," I confess.

"You fucked yourself with these fingers." He pulls my hand to his lips. "Just like you did at the restaurant."

I stare at his mouth, watching my fingers dive inside. "I did."

"You'll never be able to touch yourself the way I do." He pulls my hand down to my thigh. "You'll never be able to find the right pressure, or glide over your swollen little clit the same way I do."

"I can," I challenge. This man doesn't know my body better than I do.

His lips float over mine. "No. You can't."

My head falls back against the wall as he pushes two fingers into me. "Yes," I whisper. "Yes."

"You're already so ready." He pulls his thumb over my clit. "You're swollen. It's not going to take much until you come all over my hand."

I want to breathe. I want to feel. I want to give myself to this pleasure. "I'm close."

"I know." His lips claim mine as he applies the slightest pressure to my clit sending me racing into the clutches of an intense climax.

TWENTY EIGHT
ALEC

"Can you stay with me tonight?"

Fuck my life all to hell. Seriously. Fuck it all.

"Your bed isn't big enough for the two of us." I whip my head to the side to look at her. She still has the post orgasmic glow in her eyes. She came so hard when I had her pressed against me in the store. Now, I'm sitting in the back seat with her, while Gabriel drives us to her place. That's where I have to leave her. It can't be any other way.

She smiles slightly. "It's big enough."

"There's no way in hell it is. You'd have to sleep on top of me." I chuckle at the thought, even though there's nothing in the world I wouldn't give right now to crawl into that bed with her.

She pulls her hands through her hair, straightening it. "Can we stay at your place?"

I've always dreaded hearing those words from a woman I'm fucking. It's different this time though. It's what I want too. The problem is that it can't happen tonight. It can't happen tomorrow night or next week. It can never fucking happen because my life is a goddamn mess.

"I have an early meeting. I need to get up before dawn." The lie is too easy. That's because it came out under a veil of truth. I have a conference call with Hong Kong early, but I'll do it from home. My real home, not the condo I took her to on the Upper West Side.

The rejection stings her. I see it when she turns to look out the window, her reflection in the car's window giving away the deep disappointment she's trying to mask beneath a weak smile.

"We can have dinner together tomorrow." It's a weak offering. It's all I can give right now. I've never gotten to this point with a woman. They've tried to latch on and I've always run. I've been able to cut them off without a backwards glance but I can't with Libby. I have to figure this shit out.

"I have plans with some of the cast tomorrow." She doesn't turn to look at me.

I can't stand the distance. After watching her come I need her to be close. I only have a few more minutes before we pull up the curb in front of her place. "Is it a celebration? Can I come?"

Her head darts back, a small grin pulling at the corner of her beautiful mouth. "No. You're not invited."

"Really?" I lift a brow. "Why not?"

She licks her bottom lip. It's a thoughtless gesture but it wakes up my cock. The selfish part of me wanted to push her to her knees back at the store so she could blow me. I've been craving the softness of her mouth since she took me at the condo. I need it again. I have to have it soon.

"It's not for investors." She pulls air quotes around the phrase. "It's for the common folks."

"You're a common folk?" I reach out to touch her leg. "You're not common."

She inches closer to me, allowing me the room I need to move my hand closer to her core. "What am I then?"

"You're perfect." I lean in, pulling my lips across hers. "You're everything, Libby."

"I'm not." She pulls back to rest her head on my chest. "But I like that you think so."

* * *

"We're doing auditions for the solo today. It's nice of you to make an appearance," Sharma says through gritted teeth as I step off the elevator.

Christ, this woman can't stand me. "That's what you called me down here for?"

She doesn't pull her gaze from the tablet she's holding. "You said we should leave the solo in, so I thought you'd want to be here to help choose the girl who gets it."

Fuck. Just fuck.

I haven't had a chance to talk to Libby about this yet. "Do they know there's a solo?"

Her eyes rake over my face. "Of course they know."

"Of course they know?" I parrot back. "What the hell does that mean?"

She rolls her eyes at me. "They need to prepare so we gave them the song they'll be singing."

Libby hasn't said a word about this to me. Not one single word. I can't say I'm surprised. It's not like we've been focused on the show when we've been together. I can't exactly call her out into the hallway either. She made it clear that she wanted to keep this thing between us private. I'm not going to take that away from her. I'll just have to sit through these fucking auditions and figure out a way out of this.

"We need to start." Sharma holds open the door to the rehearsal space.

I close my eyes, straighten my jacket and walk into the room.

"Ladies," Sharma claps her hands together as if she's trying to get the attention of a group of pre-schoolers. "We're ready to start. Mr. Hughes has graced us with his presence."

I shoot her a look before taking a seat at the table. I know I need to look up. I know I need to find Libby's face.

"Libby Duncan will go first." The stage manager calls from the left.

I draw my eyes up from the table. She's there, standing in the middle of the open space. Her hair is pulled back into a high ponytail, her body wrapped in a simple blue dress. Her gaze is cast to the floor. I can tell from the way she's clutching her hands together that she's nervous.

Look at me, Libby. Christ, just look at me.

As the music starts, her beautiful, warm voice fills the room. I pull my hand to my chest. I lean forward and I stare straight into her eyes as she captivates the entire room.

TWENTY NINE
LIBBY

I'm smart. I finished high school before everyone else that I went to grade school with. I was
more than a year ahead of them. I went to college early. I graduated at the top of my class.
I've always been book smart. I'm sure as hell
not smart when it comes to men.

Alec Hughes neglected to tell me about the
auditions for the solo. I thought I knew why. I
thought he had nothing to do with it. When
Sharma announced that there would be a solo,
she explained to us that it was at the insistence
of the writers. I wanted to get it on my own.
I didn't want his influence to sway anyone. I
thought I could have my solo and Alec too so I
didn't mention it to him. I didn't want him to
call Sharma and insist I get the part.

I had rehearsed the song over and over
again, on the subway, in the store and in my
room. I was prepared, I was ready and then

he walked into the rehearsal hall. I didn't look at him until I was already singing. It broke me. Not because I was so completely over-whelmed with his presence but because I was surprised he was there. He never gave me a warning he'd be sitting at that table. We never discussed it.

"I still can't believe I got the solo." Claudia reaches to hug me before she sits across from me in the café. "Can you believe it, Lib?"

I can't. I can't fucking believe it. I know I told Alec that I didn't want a solo. I know I swore up and down that it would put a target on my back and that I'd be known from this day forward as this season's piece of ass, but once it became a reality, I wanted it. I really wanted it and it's tearing me apart that I didn't get it. "You deserve it." I don't know if I believe the words, but the decision is done.

"Alec Hughes couldn't take his eyes off of you." She slides a cup of coffee across the table towards me. "I thought you'd get it for sure."

Me too. I really did and not just because Alec was part of the group who made the final decision. I thought it was because I was the best. "You did a really good job, Claudia."

"Thanks." She leans back in the wooden chair crossing her long legs. "My parents are going to fly out for opening night."

If it would have been anyone else, it wouldn't sting this much, right? Why does it have to be one of my closest friends? I'm going to have to listen to her talk about it over and over again. I'm not a jealous person. I don't tie myself up in knots if people have nicer things than I do. I don't let it weigh me down if someone is happier, but this. This is the one thing I truly wanted and now I'll never have it.

"When they get here, do you want to come over to my place for dinner?" She's on cloud nine. "I really want them to meet you. I've talked non-stop about you for the past year."

I pull a smile from somewhere and flash it across my lips. "I wouldn't miss it for the world. I'd love to meet them."

"I finally feel like everything's going my way." She claps her hands together and bounces to her feet. "I need to take off. I'll text you later, okay?"

I nod as she turns on her heel, races out of the door with my dreams in her hand.

* * *

"We should talk about the solo, Libby." I feel his hand on my elbow before the words hit me.

I turn slowly. This isn't like the last time he showed up here at Whispers of Grace. This time the shop is bustling with customers. Jax and Ivy are upstairs. I'm not alone. I'm grateful for that. I don't know what I would say to him if it were just the two of us. "I'm working."

He rubs his hand over his forehead. "Do you get a break?"

"I don't." It's not a lie. I have a quick shift today and besides there isn't any time for a break. Ivy's interview with a fashion magazine has upped the store's sales by more than double. We can't keep up with the constant stream of people coming in to buy her designs. She's given me more shifts, which I'm grateful for. It keeps my mind off my sinking Broadway career.

"Alec?" Jax's voice calls from the corner of the store. "Hey, Alec."

His head spins towards Jax, which gives me the escape, I've been longing for. I move quickly towards a customer who launches into a sweet story about a ring he wants to buy for his wife.

I try to focus on my work. I need to. I know it's just a matter of time before the store clears out, the closed sign is turned on and Alec and I discuss the solo.

THIRTY

ALEC

Whenever I've been in this situation in the past, the decision has always been clear cut. Lie. When anyone comes to me with an idea and it's wrong, I'm not going to correct them if it means I come out looking like an asshole. Who would willingly do that to themselves? I would and I am. I have to.

"I knew about the solo, Libby." I close my eyes. I close my fucking eyes because I'm a pussy. I can't stand the thought of seeing any disappointment on that gorgeous face. I can't. It's going to kill me if I know I'm the one who put it there.

I open my eyes to see her sliding closer to her door. Gabriel has strict orders to drive us around the city until I tell him otherwise. I need to fix this. I need for Libby to understand why she didn't get the solo.

"When did you know about it?"

Christ, she can't even look at me. She's playing with a loose thread on her skirt. I've hurt her. I should have talked to her about this. I should have dragged her perfect ass out of that rehearsal hall to tell her what the fuck was going on. "I'm the one who suggested it to Sharma."

"What?" Her hand bunches into a fist before it leaps to her chest. She's guarding her heart. I can see it.

I put my hand on the seat between us. I want to reach out to her but I know she'll pull back. "It was weeks ago, Libby. Right after we met. I brought up a solo. I told Sharma to arrange it."

Her chest heaves as she pulls in a breath. "You told her to arrange it because you wanted me to have it?"

It sounds logical until you jump to this moment in time when the solo is a go and Libby's not the one belting out that song on opening night next week. "That was my intention back then."

She shakes her head slightly. "I don't get it, Alec."

"I wanted you in my bed, Libby." That's the place this needs to start. It's when this twisted mess began. "I knew if I offered you a solo, you'd fuck me."

"You're saying that the part was created just so you could fuck me?"

I nod. "I'm a pathetic piece of shit, Libby. I would have done anything back then to get you to fuck me."

A small smile tugs at the corner of her mouth. "I'm not touching that."

I reach for her hand and she doesn't resist. I cup it in my palm. "I fucked up. I should have talked to you about it. Sharma was handling it all. She said she'd hold auditions for it and I knew you wouldn't want me involved."

"Why were you there that day? Why were you at the auditions then?"

"I had no idea what was going on until she told me in the hallway before you started singing." I yank her hand to my mouth, brushing my lips across her fingers. "I wanted to pull you out of the room to give you a warning but there was no time, Libby. I wasn't expecting to be there either."

She blows out a heady stream of air. "You sure go to a lot of trouble to get laid. I told you I didn't want anything."

I'm ashamed. It's not something I've felt often. I own up to what I do with women. I'm the guy that buys pussy. I may not call up a prostitute but what I've done in the past is the same. When I want a woman, when I crave her, I'll find out what she wants and give it to her in exchange for her body. "I know, Libby."

"Why didn't I get it?"

I turn to look at her face. The bruise to her ego may not be on full display but I see it. I saw it when she turned to look at me in the jewelry store two hours ago. "We agreed to a vote. Majority wins."

She nods her head in gentle understanding. "Did you vote for me?"

It tears me the fuck apart that she has to ask that. It's killing me inside that I can't tell her what I'm feeling for her. "I did, Libby. I did."

* * *

I'm not a juggler. If I was in the circus I'd be one of the tight rope walkers. They risk life and limb to cruise across a tiny thread of hope. That's what's happening in my life right now. I have a thread of hope that opening night isn't going to be a fucking disaster.

"I've arranged the car to pick up Mr. and Mrs. Morton from the airport." Lance takes another look at his legal pad. "You're sure they don't need a hotel reservation?"

"They're staying at my place." I feel my stomach wrench with the words.

"Do you want me to make a hotel reservation for you then?"

Who knew Lance could be funny? Maybe having a male assistant isn't all that bad. "That's not necessary. I have other places I can stay at if it's too crowded. "

"Alright." He taps his foot on the floor. "I was wondering about something, sir."

"No, you can't have a raise." My eyes stay glued to the contract I'm trying to skim over before five o'clock. "I pay you too much already."

He shuffles his feet nervously. "No, I don't want a raise. That's not it."

"That's good to know." I stop to look up. "What the hell has you so jumpy?"

"I know you're bringing them here for opening night of the musical."

"Thanks for the reminder."

He looks across my desk at me. "I know it's not my business, sir, but it's been years since it happened."

Christ. No. Just no.

"Don't," I hold my hand up to silence him. "We're not discussing this. How the fuck do you know about any of it?"

"Mrs. Morton, she…well, she…" he stumbles along, tripping over his words. "She explained everything when I called to confirm her airline reservation."

Of course she did. She'll tell anyone who gives her an ear. She can't shut the hell up about it. It's been five fucking years and she'll never stop. I can't do this. I can't talk to Lance or anyone about this. "It's none of your fucking business."

"If it helps, sir." He keeps talking. His god dammed lips keep moving and more and more random bullshit is falling from them. "If it helps, I think she needs to let go."

I'm the only person in the world who thinks that. I've never expressed it. Now, my assistant is standing in front of me, saying what I've wanted to say to Margaret Morton for years. She does need to let go. We all need to let go. The past is in the past and unless I can pull a fucking rabbit out of a hat, my past is about to collide with my future.

THIRTY ONE

LIBBY

"Have you ever gone on an audition and you just knew. I mean have you ever felt that a part was made specifically for you?" I try to slow my breathing down. I'm not sure the words I just threw at Claudia made any sense at all.

"Oh my God, Libby." She grabs hold of my shoulders, shaking them furiously. "Are you talking about your audition for Falling Choices?"

I nod my head, afraid to give my voice to the motion. If I say it out loud, I'm making it more real. I can't get my hopes up again. I can't believe that a part is mine only to have it slip away. I did that with the solo and although I've settled into feeling happy for Claudia about it, I don't want a repeat.

"Tell me what happened." She holds tighter to the edge of my sweater. "I want to hear it all."

I don't want to repeat it back. If I do that, I'll pick it apart and find fault in myself. I've always been that way. I'm a perfectionist when it comes to performing and I just want to ride the high I'm feeling right now. "I don't want to jinx it." I grab hold of her hands.

"That's a good idea." She nods in agreement. "Can you imagine if you get it?"

I can and I have. I auditioned for a lead role. That would mean I'd be the star of the show and it even though it's a touring production, it would give me more stage time than I have now with my part in Selfish Fate. I'd have to leave New York but the only thing holding me here is Alec and we're still moving along at the same pace we have been all along. I know it can't last forever. Men like him don't commit to anything beyond the foreseeable future. My career is my first love so I need to stay focused on that and the lead role in Falling Choices will open a lot of doors for me.

"My parents will be here next Tuesday. Do you have to work at the store that night?"

I hesitate. It's the night before we open. I was hoping to spend it with Alec. "I'm only working on my days off from the musical now."

"So you'll come meet them for dinner?"

I rub my forehead. If I see them for an early dinner I'll still have time to see Alec before bed. "Sure. I know how much it means to you."

"It means everything, Lib." She hugs me tightly. "Family is everything to me."

* * *

Family is nothing to me. Wait. That's not completely true. It's a royal pain in my ass. My father is proving that to me now.

"That's all well and good, Libby but it's not a career you're going to be able to sustain in the long term."

I pull my smartphone away from my ear. How is it possible that he can yell at me from half way across the country and it stings just as much as if he was standing directly in front of me? "It's a big deal. If I get it, it means I'll be the lead."

"If you get it?" he hisses the words out, one by one. "If you get it? You haven't even gotten it yet."

Thanks, dad. Way to burst my confidence bubble into ten million little pieces. "I have a good chance."

"You don't know that," he presses. "It's not a sure thing. If you come back to Denver, I'll give you a job."

I rub my temple, the first bite of a migraine pulling itself to the surface. The job he's offering may come with a tidy salary and a nice benefits package but it's an entry level position that I'm over qualified for. I worked for my father's company during summer breaks throughout high school and college. I know the inner workings of the hotel business. I can save him money, streamline the operation and create more jobs, but he won't listen. The only reason he won't is because I'm not his son. My brother won that crown and now sits in a plush office, pulling in a seven figure salary while doing absolutely nothing at all.

"Did you hear me?" he barks into the phone.

"It's impossible not to hear you, dad." I sigh before continuing, "I'm not coming back there. I have to see this through. You know this is my dream."

"Dreams don't pay bills, Libby."

"Thanks for the tip." I stare at my phone wondering why I answered in the first place. "I need to go. I love you." I do. They're not empty words. My dad is my dad. I can't deny that.

"I love you too and the job is yours whenever you want it."

I don't want it. I want my life here. I want all of my dreams, including the ones I have about Alec Hughes, to come true.

THIRTY TWO
ALEC

"Alec." My name is nothing more than a whisper when it leaves her mouth and presses into mine. She's on top of me, her hair falling into my face, her tits resting against my chest. I'm buried completely inside of her and I'm holding onto her for dear life.

I circle my hips beneath her, pushing my cock into her beautiful body. "Libby," I say her name to replace the million things I want and need to say to her. They're all the things I should have said weeks ago but I haven't. I won't. I can't.

She eases herself up, her hair forging a path across my face and chest. I breathe in the scent. I hold it along with my breath.

"I think about you all the time, Alec."

Fuck. Please, God. Not now. Please.

The words rip through me. Her face is so beautiful. She's leaning back, her hands resting on my thighs, her beautiful body on full display. This isn't fair. It's not fucking fair. "I think about you too."

They're five simple words that can't convey their true meaning. When I wake up, Libby's face is there, first in my mind. As I wander through my day, she's there in my thoughts. I look at the pictures on my phone dozens of times a day. I sit outside the rehearsal hall knowing she's inside. I want to go upstairs and watch her rehearse. I want to encourage her, applaud her, and celebrate who she is. I want to steal her away from that shitty apartment she lives in and move in here with her. I want this to be my life.

"I love having sex with you."

The words are strong and filled with need. "I love it too," I whisper into the calm space between us. "Fucking you is incredible."

She shifts her hips slightly so there's pressure on my balls. I'm close. I can feel it. I need to slow the need. I can't come yet. I still my body.

"I haven't had that many lovers," she confesses as her hand glides across her breasts. "None of them were like you."

I knew that. It's not an assumption based on ego. I could tell by the way her body responded to mine. I could tell by the way she tightens when I slide myself all the way in. She's not used to the width or the length. It's almost too much. The faint flash of pain that grazes across her eyes told me everything the first time.

"I've had many lovers," I stall my breathing to moan when she rocks her hips slightly. "None of them were like you."

A smile covers her mouth and flows into her eyes. "I'm different?"

She has no idea. "You're not like anyone, Libby."

"I like that." She arches her body, pulling her hips back and then slamming them forward again.

I can't take it anymore. I grab her face with my hands, tugging it to me. "Libby, I…" I lose my voice in her kiss. Her lips are soft and plush. She pulls my bottom lip between her teeth as she fucks me hard, her body grinding into mine.

I need the control. I have to have it. I wrap one arm around her waist and in one quick movement she's on her back. I hover above her, staring down at her. "Fuck, you're so beautiful."

Her lips part. "Hard, Alec. Fuck me hard."

I reach for her hands, pinning them to the bed above her head. I need her like this. I need to see this vulnerability one last time. I fuck her tenderly. I fuck her with deep thrusts. I fuck her until she screams out my name and then I follow her into my own intense climax.

* * *

"Are you seeing anyone else?" Her voice is barely there as she pulls on her heel.

"What?" I spin around to look at her. "What did you just ask me?" I know what I heard. I fucking know what she asked me. Christ. I'm such a fucked up bastard. This is when I tell her. This is when it all comes out into the open and she runs away.

"You never want me to stay." She pats the edge of the bed. The room is silent except for the rhythmic sound. It's dim and smells like sex and lust. It's the place I never want to leave.

I look down. The words aren't there and it's not surprising. I haven't thought it through. I've always fucked them and sent them on their way. I never answer questions like this. I can't answer them now.

"Are you used to being alone?" It's an out. She's thrown me a fucking life preserver because that's who she is. "Is that why I can't stay?"

I move towards her, dipping my head to run my lips over her forehead. "I've been alone for a long time. I'm not close to many people."

Her face softens when I sit beside her. She pulls my hand onto her leg. "Where does your family live?"

"My family?" I look down at her.

"Your parents? Your siblings?"

I trace my hand along her jaw tilting it so her eyes meet mine. "My parents live in Greece."

"Did you ever live there?" Her brows pop with the question.

I smile and lean against her. This is how it should be. It should be quiet conversations about life and family. "I've always lived in New York. This is my home."

Her hand darts to my arm, twisting it slightly. Her eyes scan my watch. "I should go home. Tomorrow is opening night. I need to be at rehearsal early."

I pull her hand to my mouth, soaking in the scent of her skin. It all changes tomorrow. This is my last chance to tell her. Once we're in the theatre, and the curtain rises, Libby Duncan will be lost to me forever.

"Alec?" Her head dips down trying to catch my gaze with her own. "What's wrong?"

I look up, the lump in my throat making it impossible to swallow. "You mean so much to me, Libby."

She reaches up to cradle my cheek within her soft palm. "You mean a lot to me too."

I lean forward, pull her head to mine and kiss Libby Duncan for the very last time.

THIRTY THREE
LIBBY

It's opening night. This is the point where my dreams are finally a reality. I'm not the lead, I didn't get the solo, but I get to dance and sing on the biggest stage of my career. Previews were fun and a lot of hard work, but they don't compare to what's about to happen.

I'm dressed in my costume. The tiny white skirt floats around my thighs. The white blouse is buttoned just enough to allow my breasts to spill out. I look like a wicked angel, which is actually the point. The entire chorus line is gathered around me. I should be celebrating with them. I should be soaking in the glory of achieving something many people don't, but I can only think of one thing.

Alec Hughes.

He's a liar.

When I asked about others, he panicked. He's a master at hiding it, but I saw the fear there, between his brows. I saw the way his jaw tightened. I saw the hesitation. He didn't answer my question.

When I asked about his family, he was confused. I had to clarity the point.

When I went back to his place, after he'd dropped me at home, it all made sense. I left my phone there lost within the sheets. He'd thrown it there when he pushed me down to eat me. It stayed there when he pulled me on top of him and slid his body into mine and we'd forgotten it there when he rushed me out to the car to take me home.

Jade wasn't home so I couldn't call him to ask about my phone. I'd run downstairs, hopped in a cab and raced back to his condo on Central Park West.

"Mr. Hughes isn't here. He's never here overnight." The doorman had said. "He doesn't live here."

He's doesn't live there.

Alec Hughes is a fucking liar.

"Libby," Claudia's voice breaks into my darkness. "Look what I have."

I stop and stare. It's there in her hand. It's the proof of my need to come to this city. It's validation for all my hard work. It's the playbill. "Can I see it?"

"I got this one for you." She places it in my hand with all the care one would take when handing over a newborn child to its mother.

I greedily open it, thumbing through the pages until I find my face. I can't see it. My eyes fill with tears. "Oh my God," I whisper into the backstage noise. "Oh, Claudia."

"I know, right?" She pulls her arm around my shoulder. "We made it, Lib."

I run my hand over my face, reading the details of my biography. "This is real."

"It's totally real." Her lips graze my cheek. "You should keep it as a reminder of your first night on Broadway."

I nod as I leaf through the pages, stopping to read about my cast mates. You'd think that we'd all be good friends after working so tirelessly for so many months but there is so much competition and animosity that it clouds the judgment of even the kindest souls.

"What is this?" I hold out the playbill for Claudia. "Who is this woman?"

She pulls the edge closer to her, taking the time to read through the page. "I have no idea. It says the show is dedicated to her. Isn't that Alec Hughes standing next to her in that picture?"

It is Alec. It's his face. It's from years ago, but it's definitely him.

"Quiet." The stage manager waves a finger at everyone backstage. "They're doing a dedication."

Claudia shrugs her shoulders as she wraps her arm around my waist.

"Ladies and gentlemen, I'd like to introduce, Margaret and David Morton," Randall Myers, the producer I rarely see, hands a microphone to a woman whose face I can't make out. She standing next to a man who shares the same hue of gray hair that she does.

"We are delighted to be here." The woman's voice is soft and anxious. "We are actually standing in for our daughter, Natasha, who couldn't make it tonight. She's a bit under the weather."

The entire theatre is silent as she continues, "I'm...well...me and my husband are so grateful that our future son-in-law saw fit to invest in this brilliant production. Alec Hughes knows how much Natasha loves the theatre and this is his gift to her."

* * *

"You two need to get ready. The show starts in five." One of the stagehands peeks into the ladies' washroom, his eyes darting from where Claudia and I are standing to the empty stalls.

"We'll be right there," she barks the words at him. "I can't believe you fucked Alec Hughes."

I told her. I had to. After hearing that woman's speech I knew I couldn't go onstage without releasing some of the frustration that is brewing within me. "I don't get it, Claudia. Who the hell turns the other cheek when their fiancé is out fucking half of Manhattan?"

It's an exaggeration. I won't qualify it as slight, because I have nothing to judge by. I know that Alec fucked me. I know he's fucked women in the other plays he's invested in and I imagine he's fucked hundreds of other women. It's not a secret. His reputation precedes him, in the most negative of ways. How can any woman sit back and allow that to happen?

"It's not about her." Claudia pulls my hair into place behind my back. "This is so not about her, Libby."

"What do you mean?" I spin around sharply. "It's all about her. If I knew about her, I wouldn't have done it."

"No." Her hands firmly grip onto my shoulders. "This is about you. This is about him. This is not about her."

She's right. Alec is responsible for his own actions. He's the one who sought me out. I'm the one who willingly crawled into his bed. We made love together. I can't blame anyone for my choices but myself.

That's not going to stop me from giving him hell the moment the curtain closes tonight.

THIRTY FOUR
ALEC

I'm a coward. I'm a fucking coward. I stared at her the entire time she was on stage. She was flawless and perfect. She held her own with grace and composure. No one in the audience could have known what was brewing within her.

I watched by the dressing room door as her friend rushed to her with a playbill. I saw the tears in her eyes when she saw her face within it. I watched with regret as she listened to Margaret's speech. I stood there wishing I could shield her from it and knowing there wasn't a fucking thing I could do.

It was a fitting end to my day from hell. Listening to Natasha's parents lay all their sentimental bullshit on me was more than I could stomach. I'd left the apartment early, heading to the condo to rest on the sheets that still smelled like Libby.

SOLO

My world shifted when the doorman stopped me. Libby had come back last night for her phone. Libby had been looking for me. He told her. He fucking told her I don't live there.

The right thing to do would have been to take her phone to her and face my past. I froze. I took off my clothes, got in the bed and slid onto the sheet where she had been. I breathed in the lingering scent of her skin, closed my eyes and cried.

I cried for what I lost five years ago.

I cried for what I'm losing now.

I'm falling in love with Libby Duncan. I didn't want this to happen. I knew it couldn't happen because it would end just like this.

"Alec?" Margaret's hand is on my shoulder. "We should go back to the apartment now."

I turn around slowly, my eyes studying her face. She's aged since I saw her months ago. It's that way every time she jets back to London to live her life. It's a life that's filled with society dinners, high tea with politicians and weekend trips to France and Italy, all on my dime. She thinks she can bury the pain beneath the connections to people she deems important. She believes the reality of the situation will stay hidden behind a mask of a false smile. She's never dealt with what happened five years ago. I've never forced her to.

"I have something I need to handle here, Margaret."

Her brow furrows and a flash of disappointment washes over her blue eyes. "You know that we like to watch the performance back altogether as a family."

I'm not part of her fucking family. It's time for us all to face that. "I won't be watching this year. You and David can go ahead."

"If this is about one of your little friends…" She stops to take a heavy swallow. "If this is about one of the women you take to your bed, you know I won't stand for that."

She won't stand for it? She won't fucking stand for it? "We need to talk about things."

"What things?" she spits the words out with heavy disdain. "You know where your responsibilities are. Don't try and run away from them again."

Guilt is a bitch. It wears down the soul. It's been the burden I've been carrying with me since I was twenty-five-years old. "I'm not running from anything. I'll always provide for Natasha."

The question that's been stuck between us since the day it happened is sitting on her lips. She's not going to ask it. She won't ask it. I've always known that. "Natasha needs you. We all do."

They all need my money to live a life that affords them the chance to escape from their pain. "It's time things changed, Margaret."

She pinches the bridge of her nose. "What things?"

"This isn't the time or place." I look around us. The cast of Selfish Fate is milling about, rejoicing in the victory of a successful opening night. "I'll be home in a few hours, we can talk then."

"We don't need to talk." She takes a step towards me, her hands darting to my shoulders. "You're just feeling overwhelmed from the stress of tonight. It's a glorious musical, Alec. You've done such a good job."

It's so fucking pathetic. She thinks I'm oblivious to the fact that she can't stand the sight of me. It's why she ran off to Europe with her husband in tow five years ago. I'm her worst nightmare come true. Every single time she looks at me, she's reminded of what was taken from her. "Go back to the apartment, Margaret."

She'll run back there with David and they'll watch the performance he recorded back. They do it each time a show I invest in opens. She'll critique the casting choices, shred to pieces the musical numbers and talk about what could have been done better. I don't need to hear it. I don't want to hear it. I'm done listening to her criticize every choice I've ever made.

She leans forward brushing her red tinged lips against my cheek. The gesture is hollow and cold. "We'll take care of things there until you get back."

I nod. They'll take care of her until I get back. That's what she means. We both know it.

THIRTY FIVE

LIBBY

"You were great tonight, Libby."

I turn towards his voice. I don't recognize him immediately. My head is a jumbled mess from what happened last night when I went to see Alec. Add to that the words of the woman who spoke on stage right before the curtain went up and I can barely string together a sentence. "Thank you," I offer in polite response as I search my memory for his face.

"I thought you did a great job."

The compliment is welcomed even if I can't instantly identify the source. "It's a great musical."

His brow cocks slightly. "I hope you don't feel it's better than Falling Choices?"

That's it. I remember now. He's the producer, Garry. "I love Falling Choices." I do. I've been waiting to hear back after my audition. I had to stop checking my phone every few minutes waiting for a call because it was too distracting.

"I tried calling you several times earlier today but it kept going to voicemail." He pushes his hands into the pockets of his pants. "I know opening days are killer."

I didn't answer because my phone is on the bed in the fuck pad of a man I thought I was falling in love with. "It's been a crazy day." That's an understatement.

"This is very unusual for me." He shuffles his feet against the tile floor. "I wouldn't normally come to an opening night to deliver this news but I had tickets to the show."

News? I fist my skirt in my palms to stop from throwing my arms in the air. He wouldn't come backstage to tell me that I don't have a part. That's not the way it works. He wouldn't have tried calling me all day if he was going to tell me that I didn't measure up. This is it. Please let him say what I want him to say. "What news?" I'm shocked by how calm that sounded coming out of my mouth.

"We think you're perfect for the part of Megan."

It's the lead. The part I wanted. The part I love. "You do?"

His voice lowers. "I realize this is highly unusual but we'd need you to come on board right away. Rehearsals start in two weeks."

"I'll be there." I force a smile through a crowd of mixed emotions. "Just tell me when and where and I'll be there."

* * *

"I'm sorry I didn't tell you about her." His voice carries over the music in the club.

I thought I could escape this tonight. I thought I'd have time to rejoice in the success of our opening night with my cast mates. Early reviews are good and although they are raising their glasses of wine and mugs of beer in toasts to Selfish Fate, I'm quietly celebrating my own future with the touring company of Falling Choices. I'm moving on. I'm taking on a role that will pull me away from Manhattan, from Alec and from what could have been.

"Libby." His hand is on my arm. "I need to talk to you."

I don't care what he needs. I want him to go away and take all the lies with him. "I don't want to."

"Look at me, please." His voice cracks. "This is important."

I spin around, instantly regretting my choice in wardrobe when his eyes fall to my breasts. The dress I'm wearing is revealing. It's meant to grab the attention of anyone who can help me forget Alec. Now, that I'm standing in front of him, I feel as though I'm bare. Every part of me feels exposed. I pull my hands over my chest. "What do you want?"

"I know you're upset with me." He holds up his hand, my smartphone resting in his palm. "I know what the doorman told you."

The doorman? The small detail about Alec not living at the condo seems insignificant now. It's only a small piece of the puzzle. The speech about the musical being a gift for his fiancé is ripping me into shreds.

"Thanks for bringing my phone." I reach to pull it from his hand. "I'm going to party with my friends now."

"You're not going to let me explain this at all?" He pushes his hands into the pockets of his pants. "I want to try and explain."

I trace my index finger over my chin in a thoughtless gesture. "You're engaged, Alec. What could we possibly have to talk about?"

"It's not as simple as that." He leans against the bar. "It's very complicated, Libby."

"I don't know what's complicated about it." I pause. "You have a fiancé who is apparently fine with you being a fucked up cheating asshole. I didn't ask to be part of that and I'm not going to be again."

He bows his head as if the words have pierced his skin and he's trying to absorb the sting. "She doesn't know I sleep with other women, Libby."

That's impossible. There's absolutely no way any woman who lives in this city is oblivious to what Alec Hughes does. It's not a secret. He's been photographed with dozens of different women. The rumors are always just a step behind him. He's overt when he comes on to women. I've been witness to that myself. "There's no way in hell she doesn't know what you're doing behind her back."

He leans forward, one of his hands moving to rest on the edge of the bar. "She doesn't know, Libby. She can't know. She's been in a vegetative state for the past five years."

THIRTY SIX
ALEC

When you give voice to something as fucked up as this, it gives it merit. It's not that it makes it seem more real. It's always been real but now as I wait for the elevator that is bringing Libby up to my place, I feel a pang of something that I can't place. Regret is always there, so that's not it. It might be sadness. It feels more like hope though.

"Hi." Her voice is soft and tentative the moment the elevator opens.

I want to reach out and embrace her. She looks misplaced and nervous standing at the entry to my home. This is my home. It's the home I come to every night. It's the place I've lived for the past six years. "I'm glad you came."

She nods while her eyes search the room behind me. "Are her parents here?"

It's a valid question. I didn't have the emotional energy to explain to Libby too much last night but I had filled her in on why I needed to wait until this morning to have her come by. I needed the window of time to move Margaret and David to a hotel. The discussion wasn't pleasant. Margaret had cried and blamed and essentially called me a piece of shit in her fake English accent. I saw the pain she was in. She knows that I'm moving on and it's a reminder of what we all lost that Friday morning so long ago.

I motion for Libby to take off her sweater and hand me her purse. "They left an hour ago." I set her things down on a table.

She pulls in a breath, her hand jumping to her stomach. "I'm not sure why I came."

I'm sure of why she did. The pull that I've felt for weeks now is there within her too. I saw it last night when she looked in my eyes after I told her about Natasha. I saw the relief. "I'm glad you did. I'd like to sit so we can talk."

She follows me to a corner where a soft bench sits facing one of the windows that overlooks the city. I motion for her to sit first. I want her to be comfortable. I want her to understand that this is just as much about her as it is about me. I'm baring everything to her today. I haven't spoken about that day in years.

I've pushed it into a place where no one sees the pain it's caused. I've hidden it behind the cocky, aggressive attitude that gets me through my life.

"This view is beautiful." She lowers herself to the bench resting her back against the soft fabric.

I sit next to her. I want to pull her into me and hold her while I tenderly confess all my sins. I want her to see the truth within the words and I want her to understand my need to honor a promise I made when it felt as though that was my only choice.

"Alec?" Her hand drifts over the leg of my jeans. "I'm really nervous."

I scoop her hand into mine grateful for the contact. I'm even more thankful when she doesn't pull it away. "I'm nervous too, Libby. I'm really nervous."

She looks at me expectantly.

"I guess I need to start at the beginning." I lean back and cross my legs. As I do she pulls her hand free. I stare at it, hungry for the touch I just had. "I fell in love with Natasha in college. We dated for a couple of years and after graduation she moved to New York."

"She moved into this apartment with you?"

"We didn't live here at first." I swallow trying to clear the heavy lump in my throat. "I had a smaller place. We lived there together."

"When did you move here?" She points to the window.

"Not long before it happened."

"You said it was five years ago?" She shifts her feet on the floor. "That's a long time ago."

It feels much longer if I'm being honest with myself, which is something I haven't been since then. "Just over five years now."

"Do you want to talk about that day?" She's uncomfortable and there's no way I can blame her for that. I've pulled her into something that she has no reason to be in. I'm doing it to assuage my own sense of guilt over hurting her. I knew there was something special about her the day I met her in the elevator. When I felt myself falling for her, I should have stopped then. I should have sat her down and explained all of this before things spiraled so far out of control.

"We were staying at a house that my parents own in the Poconos." I pull my hands together. "Natasha had never been but she wanted me to take her there when I proposed."

Her eyes widen. "It's a romantic place."

223

Those were Natasha's exact words when we talked about getting engaged. She had orchestrated the entire thing. She was a perfectionist and I wanted to gift her with the proposal of her dreams. We shopped for months for the perfect ring before deciding to have one custom made. We talked endlessly about where and when I should pop the question and it was Natasha's idea to do it in the house in the Poconos on my twenty-fifth birthday.

"It was romantic," I acquiesce. "The day after the proposal is when the accident happened. That's the day I lost Natasha."

THIRTY SEVEN

LIBBY

"If it's too hard we don't have to do this right now." I reach up to take the bottle of water he brought for me. I had asked him for something to drink after he talked about the proposal. It wasn't that it stung. It just sucked something out of me. I felt parched and weak but most of all I felt smothered. I still feel that. Listening to Alec talk about the woman he loved, or maybe still loves, is making me aware of how deep my feelings for him actually are.

He lowers himself down onto the bench again. "It's important for us to do this."

"Then I'm listening."

"I had just taken over my father's business back then." He sighs before he starts talking again. "I was young and very hungry so it consumed me. I spent hours at the office chasing his approval. I wanted to do everything exactly the way he would."

"I understand." They're not empty words. I do understand. I felt that same need to please each time I stepped foot into my father's offices.

A weak smile pulls at the corner of his lips. "It's the same for you with your dad."

I nod, not wanting this to turn into a conversation about our mutual feelings of failure in the eyes of our fathers. "You took a break from work to go to the house in the Poconos?"

His eyes level back on my face. "I did. Natasha wanted to get engaged then so I took a few days away but I was still on the clock. I was working even when I should have been focused on her. She wanted to talk about the wedding. She was excited to make plans."

I hear the pain in his voice. I see it in the way he's resting his head in his hands. "What happened that day?"

"She wanted to go on a hike. I'm not that guy. I don't go outdoors just for the sake of being outdoors. "

I smile at the confession.

He straightens his back and sits up. "She got angry that I was making calls and said she was going on her own. I didn't stop her. I didn't even say goodbye to her. I just waved a hand after the door slammed shut."

I watch in silence as his hand moves towards me stopping mid-way between the two of us on the bench. I reach for it. He needs this. I need it before I hear the next words that come out of his mouth.

"It got to be late. I didn't realize for hours that she hadn't come back. "He turns to look directly at me now. "I called the police and anyone I could think of at that point."

"Did it take long to find her?"

"No." His voice sounds distant even though he's sitting right next to me. "Another hiker found her. She'd fallen and hit her head. There was blood. She never woke up again."

I bite my lip to ward off the tears when I see his lips quiver. "I'm so sorry."

"I had her brought back here." He lifts his chin toward the window. "To New York. I knew she'd have the best care here but there's nothing. She's never been the same."

"They've never been able to help her?" I ask, knowing that it's only reiterating what he just said. He's rich. His family is very wealthy. They must have used every resource available to try and help her.

"She isn't there anymore." His voice is soft as his hand sweeps over his body. "Her eyes open but she's not in there."

I don't say anything because I don't know where I'd find the words. I can't imagine the emotional torture that he's been living with. Loving someone whose body is there, whose face you can see but whose spirit has been taken away.

His mouth tightens into a thin line. "I've fought with her parents for years over her care. Natasha and I never spoke about what ifs. I couldn't make a decision I didn't feel was what she wanted so she's been living here, for all this time."

I'm not as shocked hearing the words now as I was last night when they tumbled out of his mouth at warp speed. "Why isn't she in a facility?" I'm not sure that's the right word. "I mean is she comfortable here?"

"Most of the apartment is dedicated to her care." He nods towards a long hallway. "I hired someone to coordinate everything. Her name is Jasmine. She takes care of everyone's schedules. There are caregivers here around the clock. A doctor visits her every day and if any other needs arise, she's taken to a hospital immediately."

He's thought of everything. I'm not surprised. He's very much in control of every aspect of his life.

"I considered having her placed in a facility." He scrubs his hand over the back of his neck. "Her parents wouldn't hear of it."

"Has her prognosis changed at all since it happened?"

"No." There's no hesitation in his answer. "She'll never recover. Never."

I want to ask what that means for his life. I want to know if that's why he's the abrasive, pompous asshole he was when I met him. I want to push about how that impacts us.

"Meeting you has changed so much of my life, Libby."

I hold my breath as I wait for him to continue.

"It's made me see that I can't keep living the way I have been. I can't. I need to let Natasha go." His voice cracks at the admission.

"How do you do that?" It's a genuine question.

"One step at a time."

THIRTY EIGHT
ALEC

She hasn't gotten up and walked out the door yet. I can't fucking believe it. I feel like dropping to my knees to tell her how grateful I am that she's still here.

"Why didn't you tell me sooner?"

I turn to look at her. There are tears in her eyes. They've been hovering there since I told her about Natasha's fall. I saw her chest draw in when I explained why Natasha lives here. She's too soft and kind for her own good.

I scratch my head, needing a minute longer to pull at the right words together. "I didn't want you to judge me."

She tenses, her bottom lip jutting out. "Did you think that I would?"

Since the accident happened, every single person who knows about Natasha judges me. The whispers about how I need to stay faithful and committed to her haven't been muted at all. "Libby." I hold out my hand hoping she's going to grab hold of it.

She looks at it, before her eyes move to my face. "Alec, I wouldn't have judged you."

I'm just about to pull my hand back when she places hers into it, pulling her fingers through mine. "Many people do, Libby."

"Those people don't understand." She inches closer to me on the bench. "I think I understand."

The fact that she's still here tells me she understands. The look in her eyes says the same thing. "I think you do too."

"Do you want to tell me about her?"

I do. Of course I do. Natasha was an important part of my life. Libby is too. I want to share all the details of my life with her but I don't know where to draw the line. I'll start at the most obvious place. "She loved Broadway."

Her eyebrows spike. "Was she an actress?"

"No." I laugh at the notion. "She was in finance but she always wanted to go to a play on Broadway."

"She never did?"

There's no way Libby can know how deeply that question shreds me. "She kept asking me to take her and I was always too busy with work. I promised I'd take her when we got back from our trip. We had the tickets but then she fell."

Her head darts down to hide her reaction. "Is that why you invested in the musical? It was because of her?"

This is hard. It's so fucking hard. I'm throwing my heart onto the floor. Bringing up all of this shit is reminding me of what a failure I was. "That's why. I also bought her that Tony award. It was supposed to be a wedding gift."

"That's really thoughtful." A thin smile accompanies the soft words. "What else did she like?"

"She liked helping people. She volunteered a lot. She was…" my voice stops as she pulls her hand from mine. "It was a long time ago."

She inches farther away from me on the bench. There it is. It's the realization of the gravity of this. She's finally seeing how fucked up I am and she wants nothing to do with me.

"I can take you home if you want," I offer out of respect not because it's what I want. I don't want her to leave. I never want her to fucking leave. That's why I'm showing her who I really am.

"Can I see her?"

If you would have hit me with a freight train, the impact wouldn't have compared to the shock of that question. "You want to see Natasha?"

She exhales slowly. "I would like to. Is that okay?"

I don't know how to answer that other than with the truth. I stand slowly reaching out my hand to help her up from the bench. "We'll go see her together."

THIRTY NINE
LIBBY

I think I fell in love with Alec Hughes that first day in the elevator. It didn't seem like it at the time. He was direct, and brash. He was everything I didn't look for in a man but I saw something there, in his eyes that made me want to know more about him.

Now, we're standing in a large room, the blinds are partially drawn and a woman is resting in the bed. Her eyes are closed, her chest moving in unison with the beep of a machine nearby. A tube is in her throat. She looks peaceful. She looks pained.

"Can I sit next to her?" I whisper the question into my hand.

He doesn't answer. He guides me towards the bed. His hands are clinging tightly to one of mine.

I lower myself in a chair next to her, carefully placing myself away from her bed linens.

I don't want my bracelet to catch in anything that may impact the machines. There are several, each flashing a screen filled with graphs, numbers or just a faint sound that beeps in the distance every now and again.

"She's beautiful." I mean it. I can see the beauty that Alec must have found in her when he first fell in love.

He kneels down next to me. "She was a beautiful person, Libby."

I nod as my hand cups his cheek. "I'll help you. Whatever you need. I will help."

The tears start. They are slow at first, racing a path down his cheek, stopping when they reach the slight beard that now covers his face.

"What will happen to her?" Maybe it's not my business, but it's his. I want to know. I want to know what her future will be if my future is with him.

"I've been thinking about that." His hand reaches up to pull a stray piece of lint from the sheets. "I spoke to her parents about it this morning. They're going to move here."

"To New York?" I whisper.

"Yes." His voice is strong, the tone clear. "They can live here with her and I'll move to the condo."

"Why don't they live in New York now?" It doesn't make sense. I heard the way her mother spoke about Natasha at the opening last night. I heard the pain in her voice. "Why do they live so far away?"

"They ran away after it happened." He shrugs his shoulders. "I think they couldn't handle seeing her like this."

"So they just left her with you?" It sounds cold and hurtful.

He stops to look at her face. "They told me that I was her fiancé and she was my responsibility. Margaret has never let me forget that I didn't go on that hike."

Guilt. It's such an ugly and heavy cloak to place on anyone's shoulders. "It wasn't your fault that she fell."

"It's taken me a long time to allow myself to believe that." He taps his hand on my knee. "I think that I punished myself for years because I wasn't with her when it happened."

"Is that why you never let yourself care about anyone?" It's a misplaced question given where we are. He obviously cares deeply for Natasha. He's arranged a virtual hospice in his own home. "Or was it because you still love her?"

"I'll always love her," he says without any hesitation in the words. "It's a different kind of love now."

I don't need him to explain. I reach out to touch her hand, pulling it into mine. "Thank you for letting me see her."

"No, Libby." He reaches to cover both our hands with his. "Thank you for this."

I stare at his face seeing more of him than I ever have before. This is the Alec Hughes that hides behind the arrogance and the one night stands. This is the part of him that I knew was there. I always saw it when he looked at me.

"We should go." He pulls himself to his feet. "You have rehearsal soon."

Shit. I need to tell him that I'm quitting. I need to explain why I'm walking out of his life just when he's letting me into his.

FORTY
ALEC

I think I fell in love with Libby Duncan that first day in the elevator. She acted like she didn't like me very much. It could have had something to do with the fact that I trapped her against the wall while I had a raging hard-on. That might not have been the best first impression. I saw something there in the way she looked at me. Something that made me want to tell her all my secrets and do anything she asked of me.

"I can't fucking do this, Libby." I hold her tightly to me, cradling her head to my chest. "I can't be away from you."

Her arms are wrapped around me while quiet sobs shake her small frame. "I need to do this. You know why."

I do know why. I fucking know why and it doesn't make it any easier. She's leaving because she got the lead role in Falling Choices. I half assed expected her to quit the damn thing after

I told her I arranged an audition spot for her. I knew she'd be pissed but when the anger subsided, she was grateful. She got the part because she was fucking amazing during her audition. I was there. I had sat in the back row of the small off Broadway theatre as she took the breath away of every person in the room.

"You're going to come see me a lot, right?"

"I'll be there at least twice a week." I'm the fucking boss. I can leave whenever the hell I want and now I have Lance to take over some of the slack. He's actually proving to be way more valuable than I ever gave him credit for.

"You'll call me a lot too?"

"What the hell do you think? I grab hold of her shoulders and push her back so I can look down at her face. "I'll talk to you all day if you want me to."

"I can come back if you need me." Her eyes say more than the words.

It's been a struggle adjusting to having Natasha's parents in the city. Although they've taken on her primary care, they're angry and bitter. They've lashed out at Libby more than once but she's stood her ground, keeping herself focused on all of the rehearsals she's been doing for the past six weeks for the touring company's production.

"I want you to focus on your work," I say it with sincerity. "I want you to show every person who comes out to the show why you're the next big thing."

She snuggles her body into mine, pulling her bare leg over my groin. "You believe in me."

"I'm your biggest fan." I grab hold of my naked cock. "See what a big fan I am."

She throws her head back, laughter filling the air in the bedroom. "You're ridiculous."

I push her hair back from her face. "I'm very proud of you, Libby. You have no idea how proud I am to be your boyfriend."

"What?" Her head juts up. "You're my boyfriend?"

I smile. We haven't defined what we are. We haven't had to. After I'd moved into the condo, Libby stayed with me almost every night. We talked about our past, planned for our future all under the cautious guise of a budding romance. I haven't told her how I feel. She hasn't told me, but that hasn't mattered. We both understand.

"Yes." I trace a path down her forehead with my finger. "I am your boyfriend."

She leans forward, her lips flowing softly over mine. "I like being your girlfriend."

"It comes with special perks." I push her back onto the bed and crawl on top of her.

"What perks?"

"You get to fly on my private jet." I kiss her neck, moving my tongue along her collarbone.

"What else?" she asks through a soft moan.

"You have a key to this condo."

She smiles. It's the same smile that had brightened her face the day I placed the key in her hand. "What else?"

"This," I whisper into her breast as I pull her nipple between my teeth.

"Yes." I can barely make out the word as she pushes my head down, directing me towards her pleasure.

She needs it. I want it and as I pull my tongue over her wet core, she purrs my name into the air around us.

FORTY ONE
9 MONTHS LATER
ALEC

I'm not one of those sentimental men who spend hours online looking for a romantic quote that he can post on social media to tell his girlfriend exactly how he feels. Who has time for that shit? I don't. I don't even have a fucking Facebook account. Seriously. Who besides Libby would want to be my friend? Lance, maybe Lance would.

I tell Libby how I feel from my heart and sometimes it's romantic because it's there inside of me and sometimes it comes out sounding like a bunch of bullshit. But the thing about Libby is that she can translate the bullshit into something good. She sees past the parts of me that everyone finds abrasive and cold. She sees into me, through me and that's why I love her as much as I do.

Her tour is done. Tonight was the final performance of Falling Choices. It ended its run in Denver. No. That's not some serendipitous twist of fate. I arranged that. I can do that. I wanted her parents there. I arranged that too. It wasn't easy but I got them there, they watched in wonder and they were the first to congratulate her when she took her final bow.

We are sitting outside her grade school now because Libby wanted to take me on a tour of her childhood. I couldn't resist. This is the place where she first sang in front of a crowd during a holiday pageant when she was in the third grade. It's the place she realized she was born to perform.

It's the perfect place for me to make all her dreams come true. They're my dreams too.

"I'm sorry that your musical tanked." She doesn't look at me as she says the words, but I can see the wide grin on her face in the reflection of the car's side window.

"You're not sorry." I tap her knee. "You're sorry your friend lost her job."

She twists her head to look at me. "I talked to her today. She's been going on auditions. Apparently there's a new musical in development. I might check that out when we get back to New York."

"You have the lead if you want it."

"Alec." My name shoots out from her lips. "You didn't invest in another production, did you?"

I can't tell if she's happy about the prospect or angry. It doesn't matter. "Nope. It's not mine."

Her index finger scratches right under her nose. "How do you know I can have the lead?"

"Your agent told me they called him to ask about your schedule."

"Really?" That's joy. That's pure joy in her voice.

This tour has completely changed Libby's career. She has an agent now. There are offers coming in left and right and it's not just Broadway. There are television and film roles too. She's finally getting the attention she deserves.

"You should talk to him when we get back."

"I will." She points out the window. "I used to play on those swings when I was little."

I lean over to peer out her window. "I bet you were fucking adorable."

Her head spins back towards me, our lips almost touching. "I was."

"You still are." I glide my mouth over hers, soaking in the taste of her breath.

"We should get to the airport soon." Her hand cups my cheek. I want to get back home.

"Libby." I reach down to hold her hand in mine. "I love you, Libby."

A small smile tugs at the corner of her mouth. "I love you."

"You've completely changed my life," I whisper the words into her cheek. "I can't live without you in my life anymore."

"It's the same for me." She reaches to cradle the back of my head. "You are my everything, Alec."

"I want to be with you forever." My voice cracks. I fucking knew I'd cry. Fuck.

"Me too." She pushes her beautiful mouth into mine. "Forever."

"Marry me, Libby. Just fucking marry me."

"What?" She pulls back, her eyes raking over my face. "Say it again."

"Please, Libby." I pull in a breath to quiet everything I'm feeling. "Will you marry me?"

Her eyes mirror the movement of my hands as I pull a small black box from my suit pocket. I open it slowly. A beautiful solitaire diamond sits waiting for her finger.

She picks it up slowly, nods her head and says the words I've been waiting to hear since she stepped into that elevator more than a year ago. "I will. Yes. I will."

EPILOGUE
2 YEARS LATER
LIBBY

"When mommy and daddy got married it was the most beautiful day ever." I press my lips to baby Ada's tiny forehead.

She doesn't wake. "Daddy was wearing a tuxedo and he looked so handsome. Mommy almost cried when she came walking down the aisle and saw that."

"Are you telling my daughter stories about me again?" His voice is warm and smooth.

"I am." I kiss his lips softly as he leans down to where I'm sitting in a rocking chair in the nursery of the condo.

He walks to the other chair, lowering himself carefully into it. "I was just telling Abe about his mother and how she's been nominated for a Tony award."

It still doesn't seem real. Hearing Alec say the words gives them more meaning. He'd first told me about the nomination the day after the twins were born. I was exhausted and elated from welcoming our children into the world. I didn't think my life could be more complete.

"You're going to win that award, Libby." He gently pushes his foot against the hardwood floor, causing the chair to glide back. "No one in this world is as talented as you are."

I hide my smile beneath another kiss to Ada's forehead. "No one in this world is as happy as I am."

"You're wrong about that." He cocks a brow. "I'm happier than you are."

He may be right. Alec's working less and living more now. He's given up the long hours at the office in exchange for more time with the children and me. He was with me almost constantly during my pregnancy. There had been some minor complications that had scared him early on so he adjusted his entire schedule so that the bulk of our days were spent together.

I'd worked right up until the six month mark and Alec took me to each rehearsal, watched every single performance and encouraged me every step of the way. I was the star of Crimson, the newest sensation on Broadway. Having Claudia as my understudy has only made the experience sweeter. She is there now, in my place, getting rave reviews and drawing attention to her beautiful voice and talent.

"The deal on the sale of the apartment closed today." Alec looks directly at me. "I'll be going there later this week to collect anything that I left behind."

It's been hard to talk about. Natasha had contracted an infection more than two months ago. Alec had taken on the task of helping her parents find the best doctors, even though they've never forgiven him for what happened. The doctors told us her time was limited and she slipped away one night in the hospital.

"I know that won't be easy." I reach out with one of my hands.

He grabs hold of it. "It's necessary though."

I nod. "I'll go with you. My parents will be here on Thursday to help with the twins. We'll go together."

He pulls my hand to his lips, whispering a kiss across my fingers. "Thank you, Libby. Thank you for everything."

"We're in this together, handsome." I smile as I say the words realizing how much depth they now hold. "We'll always be in it together."

"The four of us will always together," he corrects me as he kisses Abe's hand. "Forever, Libby."

"Forever."

THANK YOU!

Thank you for purchasing my book. I can't even begin to put to words what it means to me. If you enjoyed it, please remember to write a review for it. Let me know your thoughts! I want to keep my readers happy.

I have more serials and standalones on the way! For all of the information and more as well as updates, please visit my website, www.deborahbladon.com.

If you want to chat with me personally, please LIKE my page on Facebook. I love connecting with all of my readers because without you, none of this would be possible.

www.facebook.com/authordeborahbladon
Thank you, for everything.

ABOUT THE AUTHOR

Deborah Bladon has never read a romance hero she didn't like. Her love for romance novels began when she was old enough to board the bus, library card in hand to check out the newest Harlequin paperbacks. She's a Canadian by heart, and by passport, but you can often spot her in New York City sipping a latte and looking for inspiration for her next story. Manhattan is definitely her second home.

She cherishes her family and believes that each day is a gift for writing, for reading, and for loving.